TABLE 13

MIKE MCCRARY

TABLE 13

MIKE McCRARY

I'm a product of this visionary mother and father. – Kiran Bedi

Look, Pitbull is a product. – Pitbull

PART ONE

ONE
NOW

HENRY QUINN'S *life ended the moment he met them.*

Just didn't know it.

So easy to see now but impossible to know then. Still, he felt so damn stupid for not seeing what was coming, for not noticing what were probably blaring, screaming signs of things to come.

Thoughts form only to burst, dissolving into mist as his head snaps back.

The seat belt was solid. Did what it was supposed to do—stopped him from being thrown forward by the relentless momentum of the freshly crashed car. Kept him from sailing through the windshield and becoming one with a tree. But despite the seat belt's best efforts, his head raged forward, colliding with the factory-installed airbag before whipping back into the leather seat. Better than the alternative, but his neck will thank no one. Unfortunately, Henry has many wounds to deal with today.

Friends call him Hank. The people he's running from call him Hank, too.

They are not friends. They wanted something. Wanted too much.

Fluids spit and spray out from under the hood like a tragic water show. Even through the driving rain, Hank can smell the automotive cocktail. An overpowering smell of gas mixed with a slight, sanitized stink of wiper fluid. The hood of the Audi A8 has been shoved back toward the windshield, looks like a crumpled napkin after a finished meal.

An unforgiving tree stares back at Hank through spider-webbed cracks in the windshield. Rain streams down the bark. Feels like the tree is laughing at him. He can almost make out a face in the bark. Hank extends his middle finger. Letting the tree know who's boss around here, even though he can't feel anything in his hands.

They—the not-friends of Hank—said their environment was a product of them. Not the other way around. They asked if he was a product of everything beyond his fingertips.

TABLE 13   5

Even after all that's happened, Hank still has no idea.

Thunder cracks. Lighting streaks. The storm pours in buckets over the wreckage. His mind floats. Sparks of memories. Slamming thoughts bordering on delusions. The world is a white, thick, gooey spread. Life has taken a beat to reflect upon what has happened. Upon what still can happen.

Hank breathes in. Holds it. Considers and can't decide if he wants to continue breathing at all.

Thoughts of family rip. His mom. Hints of his father. Images of smiles flash, then blur into laughter. There's the memory of drinks he had with a woman at a bar. The pang of knowing people care about him. Might be worried about him. The wind wraps around the twisted metal of the car. The world slides back to him while the car gurgles out its last bit of life. The ring in his ears has dulled. He can now hear the rattle and hum of the front tires still spinning.

Hank exhales. A slow roll of blood snakes down his forehead. A creeping, streaming streak of crimson that's nearing a tricky decision. Move down the bridge of his nose or take a detour, risk getting caught up in the eyebrow.

He remembers a blow to the head that almost ended him. Unsure how he's even alive. Hank presses the ignition, shutting down the car. Not sure why, just seems like the thing to do. There's a sharp pain in his arm. Blood soaks his shirt. He removes his seat belt. Can't believe he even had the forethought to put it on. It was hard to think straight, given his exit.

The chaos of his not-friends.

Pushing with all his strength, the door opens with a groan of steel. Hank spills out to the ground. Knees land hard, palms flat. Fingers tingle, but he can still feel the mix of pine needles and dirt peppered with blades of grass. Some form of ordinary is coming back as the car-crash adrenaline subsides. The hurt hits him all at once. Hard to parse out the pain. Impossible to identify what came from the crash, what came from them.

Screaming faces. Crazed, frenzied eyes. Primal violence.

The woods are peaceful beyond comprehension. The rain has slowed. The night sky is so dense save for the handful of stars poking holes in the dark. The moon serves as a massive spotlight shrouded in clouds for a moment. A wind blows a powerful gust, then eases into a cool breeze that pushes across his face. Feels incredible.

Hank thinks of his mom. *Get up. Move.*

He can't stay here long. They will find the car. Not sure how long he sat there. Did the wreck knock him

TABLE 13   7

out? He could have been there three minutes, could have been three hours. No way to know for sure.

Are they on their way? Which one? Maybe both.

Shoving himself off the ground, he sees the blood caked to his knuckles. Sprays and streaks up his arm. His or theirs? His legs wobble. He drops to one knee, then stands. One foot in front of the other. Brain beaten. Body bloodied. He looks back. Nothing but thick dark.

How much of a lead do I have on them?

Hank picks up his pace. Each step is needles and nails, and he bites back a scream. Pushing through the pain, he moves faster. Teeth grinding, he dodges tree limbs and sidesteps ankle-twisting holes. He's found a manageable mix of hurt and speed.

He hums a song to distract himself. One they play at work. An instrumental version of a Chili Peppers tune—something that they roll on an infinite, eclectic playlist at the restaurant. A loop of songs, but it has roughly twenty guitar and piano renditions of beloved alternative tunes. He thinks of the restaurant. Thinks of Mags. Their kinda date. Her soul-melting smile. Her laugh. It all seems like a movie. Things he's seen but didn't live.

Hank jerks to a stop.

Through the woods up ahead, there's a light cutting through the relentless darkness. Hank spins behind a tree. Feels a dull crack in his bones. His warm, quick breaths plume out into the chilly night air. Pressing his aching shoulder against the tree, he turns his body, tilting his head ever so slightly to get a better look. His stomach twists.

There's a house out there.

TWO
THEN

"HEY, MAN. TABLE THIRTEEN. SEATED, WAITING."

The sound of the familiar voice carves through the kitchen chaos, but Hank doesn't register who the hostess is calling out to.

Hopes it's him and not him at the same time.

All he knows is that he's been double sat. Some show playing down the street let out an hour ago, and the consistently robust dinner crowd is in rowdy-rare form. As rowdy as the upper crust of New York can muster anyway.

Waters must go out, drink orders taken with a smile, ask the appetizer question. Hank knows the order. Feels the tug of the tables pulling, but the chef with the powder keg ego is barking hard right now. Red-faced, booming voice sounding off about timeliness, the delicate nature of Chef's genius meal magic that's aging rapidly while plated in front of them and not on someone's wanting, paying tongue.

Hank absorbs the abuse on a routine basis.

Chef spits fire. Choppy phrases rip. "Ruined, stupid hillbilly you." Then, "You, you stupid fucking hillbilly, have ruined what would have been the best meal of someone's sad-ass life."

The smells of perfectly cooked meats and sauces swirl. Smoke wafts off the grill. Scents of things sweet and savory. Hank had thought he might get tired of how great the food looks and smells. He was wrong.

"Hank. Dude." The hostess now stands next to them. "You're up."

The waitstaff slips past them in quick, jerky pauses followed by micro-sprints. Young women and men dressed in matching stark white shirts and midnight blue pants maneuver around Hank, Chef, and the hostess as if they were rocks in the middle of a roaring river. The walls are bleach white, with gleaming chrome ovens, counters, and fire-breathing stoves lit up bright.

Tilting his head from Chef, Hank puts both helpless eyes on the hostess.

He's got nothing. Tongue tied in knots. He's been working up to courage to ask Mags to coffee ever since he started working here. He knows he should

TABLE 13   11

rattle off some smart, cute, yet snarky comment since she's semi-responsible for the number of tables he's being slammed with. She cocks her head, bounces her eyebrows, then levels him with a simple, effortless look. Hank can't hold back his smile.

"Table thirteen," she whisper-yells. "Sat."

Hank's face involuntarily turns away from her. Forced to turn away by Chef's thumb pressed under his chin and fingers on his jaw. Clearly, he is not finished giving Hank a talking-to. Chef cranks the assault up another level.

Keeping his chin toward Chef, Hank holds his eyes on the hostess. "I'm getting rocked out there."

"Sorry," she says. "It's a full-on zoo tonight."

Chef's exaggerated nouns, verbs, and adjectives roll like waves over Hank. He weathers the raging storm while keeping his eyes on the one person in New York who might know he's alive.

Maggie, the hostess. Mags, she said to call her.

The flirting started on day one. Hank has patiently waited out the relationship she was in at the time that was so plainly doomed. *Patience* is being kind. Hank's been terrified to ask her to do anything regardless of her dating status. But his courage has shown some life lately.

"The couple at table thirteen—it's those two who love the hell out of you."

"Who loves me?" he asks, nodding at everything Chef is ranting while moving in odd circles.

"They. Them." Mags laughs as she helps adjust a plate on a passing tray. "The man and woman I just sat—"

"Hang on." Hank zeros in on Chef. Makes him his world. "You're right. I'm wrong. You're the best. Much better than I deserve to work with." Chef's verbal assault weakens off Hank's acceptance of his dominance. "Your work should be treated as the rising culinary revolution that it is. We all know it. Talk about it all the time. It makes me sick that I'm failing you. I'll do better. I know it's not enough, but that's all I can give you—my best."

Chef blinks. Speechless for the first time tonight.

Mags watches on, soaking in the seamless perfection of Hank's word work.

Hank moves away quick from Chef, nudging Mags along with him. They cut through the semi-controlled insanity of the kitchen, finding a safe spot near the giant walk-in freezer. His body vibrates. His mind runs riot through the ninety million things he needs to do in the next minute and a half. Still, he wants to hang on to a second or two more with Mags. Carve out a little more time to get lost in her eyes.

"Table thirteen is on you, dude. They asked for you. The other ones might be on me," Mags says,

TABLE 13   13

flirty through the stress. "I'll get waters and take drink orders for—"

"Fair. Thank you. But ya know, you double sat me—"

"Ahhhh. I see you." She works a fake sad-girl face. "It's all too much for a small-town boy? Should I give more tables to J-Star? Bet J-Star can handle a lot—"

"No. Hell no. Please." J-Star is a ridiculously attractive guitar player who waits tables for a day gig. Hank has never asked what his real name is. "But yes, please, for the love of God, help me."

"Done." Mags bites her lip as she spins away.

Hank wants to stop her. This is it. Time to ask her. It's perfect. Bonding moment unlocked. His blood is pumping crazy off the energy. This twisted high might make it easier to do what he's been so terrified to do.

How hard is it to ask her a question?

He can't do it. He watches her walk away. If he could, he'd punch himself in the face for missing the chance. She stops. His breathing stops. She turns back at him.

"Yes," she says, taking a step closer.

"What?"

"Whatever you're too chickenshit to ask me." She shrugs. "The answer is yes."

"Coffee?"

"Coffee?" She scrunches her nose. "Love coffee, but no. No, that won't do." She grabs his shoulders. Leans in. "Whiskey after the close."

"When?"

"Tonight, dummy."

Hank's face sags. Blank stare. Clueless in formulating a response.

"You'll tell me about your writing." Mags is so close Hank looks away, hopes she can't hear his heart cranking. "And I'll tell about the horrors of being a struggling actress."

When he stumbled down this path, he didn't map out a positive response. Not sure he thought *yes* was a possibility. Sure as hell didn't think she knew that he was a writer.

Well, trying to be a writer.

"Does that work for you?" Mags tries to coax a nod out of him.

"Of course. Are you kidding me?" So desperate. Hates that he talks like this out loud.

"Good answer." They share a laugh. "Now, let's go do our shitty jobs."

Taking a beat, Mags puts on her big-smiling, guest-facing face, then spins around, pushing out through the doors. Outside the kitchen, the packed restaurant buzzes. A living, breathing thing. Pulsing energy, much like the kitchen, just a different brand of

TABLE 13   15

crazy. The doors hide all the dysfunction and anxiety from the paying customers. And boy, do they pay. A meal here is a car payment, perhaps two. Some of these high-flying guests enjoy complaining about everything, but more of them enjoy the best of New York fine dining.

This place is a destination. An experience.

A place to be seen as well as become one with a top-five meal of a lifetime. All are served up to perfection by a highly trained staff that suffers the abuses of guests and chefs in order to live in New York, pursue a dream or two, and make some bank while working a part-time job.

Big smile. Eyes closed. Deep breath. Hank silently counts to three, then pushes himself out into the war.

One more time, my friends, he thinks.

THREE

HANK CROSSES THE THRESHOLD.

Moves from the kitchen into the restaurant's main dining room. The main stage.

He beats back the fluttering joy generated by his conversation with Mags. Needs his head clear in order to get through the next few hours. Juggle the crazy. Manage the whacko.

Then, and only then, can he have that whiskey with the amazing Mags. He doesn't love whiskey—raised on low-end beer and cheap wine drunk fast in fields back home—but that inconvenient fact will not be part of the conversation tonight.

Table thirteen is up ahead.

His regulars. His only regulars. They come in every few weeks, sometimes every few months, which is the case tonight. Can't remember the last

TABLE 13   17

time they were here, but it had to be a couple of months ago. Always the same table. Hank assumes table thirteen has some special significance, maybe where they had their first date or something, but he doesn't really know much about them. Told them some joke the first time he waited on them, can't even remember what it was, and they've loved him ever since.

Table thirteen with Hank Quinn serving, please.

The manager showed him the request one day. Oddly, each time they print out a typed request, sign it, and drop it in the mail well in advance. They are strange, but Hank doesn't mind. They are always pleasant enough. Not too demanding. They like the folksy chitchat.

The woman—Gina, he thinks that's her name— always laughs at his jokes. She's eight kinds of beautiful. The guy—Nick, Nicholas. Something starts with an N—is cool, slick as hell, but flashes warmth with a kind word from time to time.

Both gorgeous humans. Look like sex and money. Maybe they work in finance or tech, or there's some deep, blueblood family cash. They are always dressed to perfection, with Gina leaning more toward a casual, hippy-cool kind of vibe. Mr. N goes full-on movie icon out of the '50s or '60s. A mixture of James Bond and Steve McQueen living large at a perpetual cocktail party. Not to mention, they tip like a dream come true.

Like the printed reservation request, there are some other strange things about them. Doesn't really bother Hank, but they have an odd way of talking. Hank picked up on it a couple of visits ago. Not horrible, and it's not all the time, but it's in the way they phrase things. It's just a little off. Hank brushed it off as him not being from around here and them being cooler than he'll ever be.

Gina spots Hank coming their way. She waves. Mr. N turns. He grins big with a finger gun aimed at Hank.

"Hello." Hank's voice even has a smile. "My favorite thirteen twosome."

Gina laughs. Even her laugh is hot. Throaty, with her eyes lit up with genuine joy.

"Thirteen?" Mr. N says.

"That's the table number, Nathan. It's how they keep track of this wonderful little world." Gina's fingers graze his hand, then lock fingers in his. "I tell them the table when I correspond."

Hank tries to stick *Nathan* into his memory bank.

"Cool, cool. I knew that. So sorry, man. My mind slips." Nathan sips his red wine. They order by the bottle, usually two. A way-too-expensive Pinot, but still not too insane considering some bottles at this

TABLE 13   19

place rival the cost of a heart transplant. "How's life, Hank?"

"Good. Great, I guess." Hank's head is still buzzing from Mags. "Can't complain."

"And who'd give a barrel of shit if you did?" Gina says. "Right?"

"We would, Gina," Nathan adds. "We would give three barrels of shit, Hank."

"Facts." They clink glasses.

Hank smiles at the oddity of his guests. He assumes they are private school, wild children with a safety net types. So removed from the planet and its reality they don't know how to interact with normal humans. Maybe there's some spectrum type of forces at play too.

"I just finished a book." Hank moves the conversation along while making a mental checklist. Other tables are waiting. "Going out on submission soon."

Hank stops, reviewing what he just said. Can't believe he let that out there. He usually never talks about writing around here. Certainly not with guests. There's a silent pause at the table. A beat too long for Hank's taste.

"Sorry," Hank says. "You're not here to hear about—"

"Oh." Gina's eyes pop wide. She squeezes

Nathan's hand tight. There's an over-the-top delight in her voice. "You're a writer?"

"On a good day."

"That's so super fucking amazing." Gina leans in, gaze like a laser.

Hank stops. Paused by the force she laid on the f-bomb.

There's a shift in her intensity. A dial turns up.

"You moved here to do that?" she asks. "To write?"

"Take your shot in big New York City?" Nathan follows up. "Not trying to be a condescending barrel of shit, but your accent doesn't scream *boy from the Bronx*."

"I'm into the way he talks," Gina says.

"As am I. What's not to dig."

"He sounds like honesty and honey."

"A combination hard to find in this sour, lying world."

"Facts."

"Thank you." Hank attempts to regain control of the table. "I'm from a small town in Texas. But what can I get you—"

"Your folks must be some proud, proud people." Gina looks to Nathan. "New York writer-man."

Nathan nods along.

Hank can't believe how interested they are. Seems so genuine. Probably isn't genuine at all—this city is

TABLE 13   21

chock-full of liars and thieves—but Hank likes it no matter what's underneath. His experience with the Manhattan elite has not been positive. Part of him thinks he shouldn't trust it, but the small-town boy inside of him wins out. That boy likes hope. That shrinking sliver inside that wants to believe people at their core are good. Of course, that theory has been put to the test.

"Parent," Hank says.

"Oh?" Gina asks. "Dead mom or dad?"

Hank winces at the question but feels cornered to answer.

"My father died a while back."

"Dammit," Nathan says with some bite. Fist hits the table. Wineglasses jump, splashing small blobs of red on the white tablecloth. He looks to Gina with hard eyes. "That's a hard thing, right?"

"The hardest," Gina agrees with eyes full.

"It's okay. My mom is still back home. I'll probably go back soon. I don't know..." Hank's mind drifts. Thoughts of his father scream. Snaps out of it, realizing he's on the clock. So much to do. This is not the Hank sharing hour. "Sorry, this is your dinner. All that slipped out—I don't get to talk about me much."

"No. Please." Nathan holds both arms out wide, signaling Hank is being ridiculous. "No. No. No."

"Hell, no, no, no. You keep going with your

words." Gina touches Nathan's hand again. "This is what we need more of. Real people using real words forming real, perfect thoughts."

"Hell, yes." Nathan laughs big, pouring more wine for Gina, then fills his own glass. "Speak it, sir."

Chef flies out from the door, finger pointed, aimed like a weapon. Gina and Nathan take note. Hank puts up a hand, asking Chef for a minute.

"Who's that fucker?" Nathan lowers his chin toward Chef, who's now shaking his head, insisting Hank come over to him now.

Gina turns around in her chair, sips her wine while studying him.

"Looks like a bit of a dick."

"Or a fucker," Nathan adds.

"Yes, but I'd argue he's screaming *I'm a dick*."

Hank chokes on his laugh. *You're not wrong.*

"I need a minute. Apparently, I've done something not right." Hank drifts away from the table. "I'll get you some more wine. On me. Well, I can't afford what you're drinking. How about a side salad?"

"You'll pay for nothing. We pay for you." Nathan's eyes bore through Chef. His words flatten, go cold. "Don't let that slab of nothing define anything about you."

Nathan's searing look and tone stop Hank for a half second. Seems extreme, out of place. But not

TABLE 13   23

unappreciated. Gina grabs Hank's arm. Squeezes surprisingly hard, stopping him from leaving. Her burgundy nails just shy of digging into his skin. The force catches Hank off guard.

There's an ever-so-thin line of crusted, dark red across her cheek. He tries not to stare. More than likely, it's wine or misplaced makeup. But in the poor mood lighting of the dining room, it almost looks like something else.

Hank glances to Nathan.

He's gripping a steak knife. The blade catches the flicker of the table's candle ever so slightly. Gina's attention turns to the air above her as if a ghost floated by. It's the music. She closes her eyes, swaying with an instrumental version of "That Funny Feeling" by Bo Burnham.

"Man, I love this song." Lost in the tune, her hand still grips Hank's arm. "Don't you?"

Hank looks back to the knife, then up to Nathan's hard stare. It occurs to Hank; Nathan hasn't ordered yet. Steak knives are only brought out after someone orders—ya know—a steak.

Did he bring his own? Is that even a steak knife?

"Hey." Gina lets go of his arm, snaps her fingers in front of his face. "Shove this into the meat of your mind." Pokes his forehead. "That dick over there only has the power you give him."

"Are you a product of everything beyond your fingertips?" Nathan asks.

Smiling, covering up how weirded out he is, Hank slips away from the table.

"We'll be right here," Gina says, topping off Nathan's wine. "Take every tick of time you need."

"You okay?" Mags slides up next to Hank as he moves toward Chef. "I got your other tables started. Drinks at the bar. Didn't order anything from the kitchen yet."

"I'm good. Thank you so much."

The strangeness of the night hangs like a soggy robe—absorbing, getting heavier with each passing second. The high of Mags. The odd conversation at table thirteen. Nathan and Gina's concern mixed with kindness with that big dollop of *what the hell?* The constant layer of pressure from everything back home.

"Whiskey later?" Hank asks.

"Try and stop me."

Mags disappears into the crowd, heading back to her post at the front of the restaurant.

Chef pushes open the door, extending a mocking hand to show Hank the way in. He wastes no time laying into him. Hank stares into his eyes. He used to look away. Down at his shoes, up at the sky, anything but directly at Chef. That only made it worse. Now,

TABLE 13   25

he stares directly at him but lets his eyes blur out so the image of this psycho isn't so vivid.

Hank plays Mag's words back over and over.

Try and stop me.

That and the image of her smile are now burned into his mind. It will get him through the rest of the night. No matter the abuse. No matter how strange things get.

Whiskey with Mags is the light at the end of his tunnel.

FOUR

"SPARTACUS," Hank calls out to the empty apartment. "Hello, Spartacus. Come on, buddy."

Grinding his teeth, he shakes the food bag as if his life depended on it.

He needs to feed the damn cat, change into something he doesn't look shitty in, attempt to temper the smell of the steak and wine that's become a part of his skin, then run bat out of hell style to meet Mags at a bar in Hell's Kitchen. They chose—well, she chose, Hank had not a single clue where to go—a place out of the sphere of where people from work might go.

Sounded like a positive sign in Hank's limited knowledge of relationships.

His cousin is letting him stay here at his apartment while his band is touring Europe. They tour

TABLE 13   27

small clubs and bars mostly. More party than tour if everyone is being honest, funded by trust funds more than record sales. Still, sounds like a good time. Hank can't argue with it. He'd probably do the same if he could. His cousin is from the rich side of the family. Hank is not.

Hank could never afford this place or any place within miles of here. Luckily for Hank, his cousin is perpetually on tour or sleeping one off at someone's place or simply not around at all. This little arrangement has worked out okay for Hank so far. He gets to stay in a nice place, in a nice part of the city, for next to nothing. There's no room to complain, but Hank hates the hell out of the idea that, after all these years, he is still taking handouts from his *cousins with money*. Cousin Ronnie was a condescending prick about the whole thing too. Loving how much Hank needed a decent place to stay and all too willing to make a show of his and his family's generosity. Always at the back of his mind is this ticking clock of when his cousin is going to burn out and kick Hank's ass to the curb.

Is that what will send me home to Mama? Do I want that excuse to go running home?

Home doesn't want Hank, and he knows it.

Just feed the cat, don't burn the place down. Those

are the only responsibilities Hank really has here. Spartacus rubs, then snakes in and out between his legs, looking up at him like he's the most important thing on this planet or any other.

"You don't love me. Your affection is dependent." Hank dishes out some food. Gets some fresh water. "But keep lying to me, Spartacus. Take what I can get."

Emptying his pockets and making his way to the shower, he stops at his makeshift office. A small table he found in the street. Wanted something that was his. He'll throw it away, hopefully, before his cousin stumbles in. A barely functioning, out-of-date laptop sits next to a yellow legal pad that's filled with line after line of what he's sure is scribbled genius. If he could only read his own handwriting. There's also a box of envelopes with half a book of stamps next to them.

Counting out some cash, he stuffs part of it into an envelope.

He'll leave it on the kitchen counter for his cousin on the off chance he blows through. Even though he's supposedly in Europe, nothing is out of the question. Time, schedules, plans, and rules don't really apply to dear cousin Ronnie. Hank envies the hell out of him for that. Still, he likes to leave Ronnie something for

TABLE 13   29

letting him stay here. Feels less dirty than straight-up charity.

Plus, he rarely gets cash tips at the restaurant. These days, especially at a place like where he works, tips are all paid out on credit cards. The restaurant then adds those to a paycheck he'll see in about two weeks. It was rough at the start, but about a month into the job, the checks start rolling and then things even out. He deposits his checks into the bank and then takes about half out in cash so he can fill his envelopes. Keeps a stash of them. Prefers the #9s.

Hank stuffs the rest of the cash into a second envelope. Puts a stamp on this one. Writes a Texas address on a label sticker, then presses it carefully on the front.

Nathan and Gina pay in cash. Tip and check. It's another odd thing they do. Always dinner. Always the same table. Always Hank. Always cash.

He checks the time.

"Shit."

He's late. Can't be late for the first date with Mags.

Is this a date?

Unclear. But he is meeting with her at an agreed upon location at a negotiated time. He's spinning. Focus fluttering. Tapping out a text, he lets his mom know there's an envelope coming. She'll protest. Text back telling him not to, then she'll call, leaving a ten-minute message about how he doesn't need to do that and everything is fine at the shop.

Hank knows that *fine* is delusional. Everything stopped being fine after his father died.

Stripping down, stumbling toward the shower, his ankle gets caught in his clinging pant leg as he works some quick math in his head. He'll have enough cash to cover two drinks a piece, maybe an appetizer, then a tip. That's a big maybe. If he gets beer and she gets whiskey, that might tilt the numbers in his favor. But she wanted this to be a whiskey thing. She'll have some brands in mind. She's cool. She'll want cool things. Cool costs.

"Shit."

During a naked shuffle back across the floor, he considers both envelopes, then peels a few bills off his cousin's money.

Into the shower he goes. No time to let the water warm. The cold blast hits his bare skin and he bites back a whimper. Soap moves fast. Hits the main areas of concern. Pits, feet, then the delicates. Doubts there's a need for fresh and clean down below. No one's visited the area in quite some time, but he's heard if you put things out in the universe, sometimes the universe responds.

He shuts off the water. Towels off in record time. Like it or not, his friends at table thirteen pop into his

TABLE 13   31

head. They waited patiently while Hank received his talking-to from Chef. When he finally got back to their table, they didn't say another word about it.

He tried to apologize, but Nathan simply raised a hand, barely looking up from the menu. He only pressed his lips together, shaking his head back and forth, letting Hank know there was no need to explain a damn thing. *No apologies necessary here tonight* was the look Gina fired off as well.

They even bought him a beer. One of them must have snuck up to the bar while Hank was busy. A tall, golden, ice-cold glass of overpriced, locally sourced hipster ale with an ironic name was sitting on the table after they left. They both ordered massive steaks, sans the potatoes, and salads. Their check—along with all that wine—was well north of five hundred.

They left north of eight hundred in crisp cash neatly stacked to the right of the beer. A mix of tens and twenties, which Hank appreciated. Cash is fun to have. Not sure why. Guess in a world where physical items are becoming rarer and rarer, it feels nice to feel something tangible in his hands. The texture on his fingertips. The heft of the stack was pretty cool. Gave some weight to his labor. Under the cash, there was a smiley face drawn on the white tablecloth in red lipstick. Hank pocketed the stack. Downed the ironically named beer in three gulps. Now, Hank and his clean, fresh feet and cleansed delicates are going on a maybe date with Mags.

Just another night in the life of a struggling writer boy from nowhere Texas.

FIVE

HANK POSITIONS himself at the bar.

Pulls at his shirt. Tight, like an out-of-style strait-jacket. He has no idea where to sit or how to sit. Nothing feels comfortable, correct, or cool. An elusive combo for Hank. After much debate, he thinks he might have picked a decent spot.

Everyone here looks like they strolled out of a skincare commercial or a steaming limited series about amazing people who aren't you. Each more gorgeous than the next. All of them belong here. All look like they are more than Hank in every way. He knows he needs to stop thinking this way, but this is where his mind goes here in New York. The aching need to tell the city he's sorry for wasting their time.

His mom's flimsy health insurance paid for him to talk to a therapist a few times after his father died.

The final verdict was Hank suffered from anxiety, guilt, and some thorny feelings of low self-worth, and in this somewhat trained therapist's opinion, Hank needed to stop doing that. Not a great mental health worker, but not entirely wrong either. So, Hank took all that clinical data and then decided the cocktail of anxious guilt, with a touch of crushing inadequacy, was perfect for what he wanted to do with his life.

Become a writer.

Hank smiles thinking about it now. So wise and so foolish at the same time. At least tonight, Hank knew enough to know he should grab a decent spot at the bar. Mags mentioned once that she likes sitting at the bar, makes her feel like she's in the mix without having any responsibilities. Hank agrees. There's an energy to most bars. A good bartender can change the world.

The team behind the bar here is made up of a bearded, six-foot-four mountain of a man and a five-foot-nothing bald woman with an *Eat the Rich* tattoo on her neck. Seems like the two of them have got the world under complete control.

Hank has moved between two stools trying to determine which is his best side. The side that will greet Mags as she enters. Sure, she's seen him all night, but this is a new light, dammit. Literally and figuratively. This is a reset. A new vibe in a new joint.

TABLE 13   35

He's changed clothes—three times—and put some shit in his hair that his cousin left behind. He really hoping this whiskey he can't afford will loosen his mind and bring his shoulders down.

He envisions how the night will go. Stories and laughs will be shared. Smiles and eyes. He knows it's silly as hell, but he holds on to this schoolboy idea about how their first kiss will go. If he's so fortunate to have the opportunity.

Is she still getting over that other guy? God, I hope she's moved on.

Is this a friend-slash coworker type of deal? That's completely cool, but not being truly sure is a tightrope he'll have to walk for a while. Hank is not a novice when it comes to matters of the heart, but he's pretty damn close. Plus, dating in a small town is plenty different than hanging with someone like Mags in the city that chews up hearts on a regular basis.

Don't think so much.

Let the world spin.

The past is the past.

That's what his mom used to tell him. It's what she said a few weeks after his father died. It's also what she said when Hank talked about moving to New York to take his shot at being a writer. Hank was terrified. Still is. He half hoped his mom would talk him out of it, but of course, she didn't. The woman couldn't have been more supportive. Pride screamed way too loud behind her eyes despite there being so many reasons why she would want him to stay home with her.

"What can I get you?" Eat the Rich asks.

Her voice is surprisingly angelic.

"Sorry." Thinks of laying out some bro-dude bullshit. Some act about how he knows soooo much about all things. Reconsiders. Resets. Clears his throat. "Can I be honest with you?"

"If not me, then who?"

"True." Hank looks to the wall of booze that stretches up kissing the ceiling. "I don't know what whiskey is cool. Not really sure what's whiskey and what's bourbon. And I'm meeting a woman here who does know. So—"

Eat the Rich puts a finger to his lips, shushing him like a child.

"I got you, Country."

With that, she glides down the bar, leaving Hank to ponder her calling him *Country*. He's worked hard to lose his accent. At least mute it some. Thought he'd done okay.

"Shit."

"Saddest thing ever," Mags says, "Alone in a bar with only your profanity."

TABLE 13   37

Hank's heart skips a row of beats. Wolf Alice plays above them. The melodic perfection struggles to be heard over the dull hum of the crowd—spikes of half-drunk laughter mixed in with full-drunk stories told with too much enthusiasm. All of it fades into the background as Hank gets lost in her smile. Slips into the abyss he's come to know and love. That space inside him that gets gone while being with Mags.

She cocks her head, waiting for some form of response.

Hank looks down. Resets. Fights to find something slick or even interesting to say.

"Hi." All he's got.

"Hello, Hank." Mags hangs her purse on a hook under the bar, staring at the empty polished wood in front of them. "Did you order yet?"

"He did." Eat the Rich slides two glasses with a healthy pour of brown liquor that glows under the light. "Good eye, this one. Angel's Envy Rye."

Mags's eyes light up, her lips press together —impressed.

Hank mouths a *thank you* to his new bartender best friend who wants to feed on the wealthy. He pulls a few bills with an eye to Eat the Rich. *This cover it?* She raises her thumb quick, so Mags doesn't see. Hank adds another couple of bills. Giving a single nod, she takes the cash, drifting on to serve the growing mass of thirsty New Yorkers.

Mags raises her glass, Hank follows suit.

"Cheers, man." The glasses clink. She takes a sip. Her face morphs, eyes closed, as if she's tasted the meaning of life. "So good."

"It is," he agrees, trying not to sound surprised. "It is good."

His knowledge of whiskey—or bourbon or rye or whatever the hell it is—has been limited by parties on deer leases by a bonfire. Usually whatever his small-town buddies lifted from their parents' liquor cabinet stored in a Tupperware or cheap plastic flasks. And where he's from, *liquor cabinet* is a generous way of saying the upper shelf of the pantry above the Fritos and Frosted Flakes.

The whiskey slips down his throat. A good burn. He gets it now. He takes another sip, trying not to think about what each sip is costing.

"Writer, huh?" Mags leans her elbow on the bar with her chin resting on her palm. "That what brought you to the big, bad city?"

"Pretty much."

"Didn't come here to be a waiter? Get yelled at by… well, everyone."

"Oddly enough, no. I don't mind being a waiter, though. The money is good, not like I take work

TABLE 13   39

home with me, ya know? Gives me time to write, I guess."

"Same." Mags shrugs. "Not a dream job, but it lets me eat and gives me some freedom to audition and all that."

"How's the acting going?"

"How's the writing going?"

"Well…" Hank teeters between the truth and being cool. "What can I say?"

"Same."

Smiles and understanding nods slide into rolling laughs.

Struggling artists trying to push the elephant up the stairs. Neither looking for sympathy. It's the game they chose to play. Cube-dwelling day jobs are plentiful and easy to find. They line the buildings of this city, row after row filled with people almost living while waiting to die. Dream following is a rough-and-tumble way to go for most. The upside is, no matter how hard the path, everything on top of everything sprinkled with all the dreams of all they ever wanted. The downside is unthinkable.

The last of the Angel's Envy slides past her lips. Mags gets Eat the Rich's attention.

"Two more, please." Mags puts down her card. "I got this one."

"No. Please, let me." Hank pushes her card back. "I

asked you—"

"Hank." Mags gently removes his hand from the card. Leans in. "Let's be honest. I asked you. I'd die of old age waiting for you to say anything. So, the least I can do is pick up a round."

She taps his forehead with the card, then places it back on the bar.

"Think about how you're going to wow me with some of that cool writer shit." She pushes off the stool, turns toward the restrooms. "And throw in something folksy material about that small town you ran away from."

"I'll do my best."

Mags touches his shoulder as she slips past him. Hank's heart races in the best way possible. Eat the Rich delivers two more drinks, takes her card, and bows before Hank as if he's the king of all things. For the first time in his life, Hank kinda thinks that he might be. Ten feet tall. A tower of Hank. He belongs here. In this bar. In this city. This world. Floating as these ridiculous yet wonderful ideas sink in.

Hank catches a glimpse of himself in the mirror behind the bar. "Well done." Raises his glass to himself, then takes a drink. Loving it all. "That is really good—"

"Hank." A familiar voice cuts through his thoughts.

TABLE 13   41

Hank turns.

Nathan and Gina stand behind him. Hank's skin tingles. Anxiety twists in his stomach. That feeling that comes from running into someone you're not sure you want to run into. They both hold fishbowl size glasses of red wine. Doing quick math, he calculates they are both at least down a bottle of vino a piece. Plus, a couple of these fishbowls.

"Hey." Hank swallows. Digs up a smile that resembles *good to see you*. "My favorite table thirteen. What are you up to?"

"We love coming here. Not as much as your place of employment. That restaurant, my lord, love to celebrate there." Gina sways back and forth. She's tipsy but in a controlled, free-floating easiness. Someone who's not fighting the winds of intoxication. She's making it work for her, turning it into her own dance. "Great spot."

"Dinner there has become a ritual," Nathan adds. "Not ritual, that sounds super cult whacko. What am I looking for..."

"Tradition?"

"Yes." Nathan snaps his fingers, frustrated he didn't land the right word. "Tradition. We eat there as a traditional, celebratory meal."

Part of Hank wants to ask what they celebrate there, but he doesn't want to extend this conversation any longer than he needs to. Really wants them gone before Mags gets back.

Nathan leans in closer to Hank than Hank would like. "She's a very pretty-pretty woman."

"Who?"

"That woman." Nathan holds his eyes, then eases back, wrapping his arm around Gina's waist like a snake. Gina nibbles on his ear. "She's the hostess, right? Really attractive person."

The odd choice of words they use. The strange way they both speak. Hank noticed it before, of course, but never really spent any time thinking about it. They are a beautiful couple, but those things that have always been off about them are so front and center now. Like an amazing painting with color choices that don't belong, hung on the wall with a frame that's chipped and battered.

"Miss." Gina snaps her fingers at Eat the Rich. An attention grabber that isn't well received. "Miss. Please get these two lovelies a bottle of whatever the fuck they are drinking. Put it on us."

Eat the Rich stares back, death daggers flying.

"Oh, no. No, thank you so much, but that's not necessary," Hank says, turning back and forth between them. "It's really expensive—not sure what things are called in this city—but really, you don't have to."

TABLE 13   43

Nathan pulls a roll of cash from his pocket. A rubber band bound bank.

Same way they paid for dinner earlier tonight. With a toss, the roll bounce-rolls onto the bar. Eat the Rich's eyes soften, but never go completely from hate to happy. There's a wilt of knowing you've been bought. The quiet conversation explaining, rationalizing with yourself that you need the money for the greater good.

Eat the Rich takes the cash, seems to do some math—how much it costs her to forget but not forgive —reaches behind her, then places a new, unopened bottle on the bar. Its tall, perfect curves contain the amber glow, taking an almost celestial quality under the bar's lights.

"Okay," Hank says, turning back to them, "that's an amazing, generous gesture, but—"

They're gone.

Nathan and Gina have vanished as fast as they arrived.

"Wow."

Hank spins back around on his barstool as Mags slides into her spot next to him. Her eyes are on the fresh bottle in front of them as Eat the Rich sets down two empty glasses with mouths open, waiting for a pour.

"Well, someone got thirsty as hell."

SIX

WALKING BACK, some stumbling, Hank finally understands the next level cheese bag *walking on air* saying that has polluted his brain for years.

Maybe he's heard it in songs.

Definitely heard his mom say *I was walking on air* from time to time when telling stories about dating his father. After he died, he never heard her say it, and Hank doesn't recall his father saying anything like that. Ever. After his passing, his mom used to say, *Captain Reality is a mean SOB, but I prefer to watch my own movie.* Hank thinks his mom might have become a little delusional with her memories of their marriage considering what happened, but Hank lets it go. What's the point?

Walking on air.

Hank realizes those words were glossing over a

TABLE 13   45

lot of ugliness reality can dump on a life, on a family, but the idea that's how she chooses to think about things is comforting in a way. How she's decided to view their time together. Hell, that might be enough to punch a hole in the dark for Hank. Even if it is a clear form of denial, so be it. So what?

If this is what she's talking about, if right now is what that's like, Hank thinks as he steals a look at Mags, *then strap on as much denial as you've got, Captain Reality.*

Part of him wants to stop. Silly to think this way. Walk away before it all goes wrong, as things always do. Always. The mild, warm hum of a buzz drowns out such self-defense born thoughts. He's helpless, completely captivated by every word Mags speaks.

The way she tells a story. Avoids sentences that start with *I* or ones heavy with the subject of *me*. She's kind with an edge. Sure, the booze, the night he's had, along with strolling under the moonlight of this amazing city are strong factors steering his perception, but being in New York just after 1:00 a.m. with Mags does have a certain airy quality.

The way she pushes her hair behind her ear. The curl of her smile.

All while dodging the potential problems of the city. Puddles, drunks, people with necks bent down and eyes locked on phones, late-night dog walkers, homeless swinging at tortured visions, lovers wandering—all the glory and gore the city has to offer.

They took the subway to Mags's building. Hank has avoided the subway as much as he could ever since he moved here. Scares the hell out of him. Didn't love the ride he took with her either—pretty much white-knuckled it the whole way—but it was the best one he's had so far. A low bar to clear, no question. His fear of the hell-like craziness of the subway can only be surpassed by his fear of the moment that's coming up soon. The fear of what to do when they get to her place.

Will there be a kiss?

Is that way too schoolboy? Not sure there are many men his age—considers himself a semi-adult—who sweat a goodnight kiss. This is New York. We're grown-ups. *Good God, man. Pull it together.*

A new question pops up.

Should he express interest in more than just a kiss?

Would a woman like Mags be offended if he didn't, at the very least, hint at the proverbial *going upstairs*? Through the magic of movies and television, he knows if she asks him if he'd *like some coffee* that means something else. Still, he's not sure.

Maybe she does just want some coffee.

TABLE 13   47

They talked about a lot of things tonight. He's fought the haze of the booze. They didn't even come close to finishing that new bottle. Eat the Rich was amazing. She scribbled *Mags* and *Hank* on the bottle, then tucked it away somewhere under the bar.

It wasn't lost on Hank that this amazing bartender did him a solid by putting both their names on the bottle. He could never match the wad of cash Nathan dropped on her bar, but he laid down the tip the best he could. The best he's ever tipped anyone ever on this planet.

Mags stops. Pushes her chin up toward a five-story walk-up.

They've reached her place.

Hank swallows hard. He'd completely lost track of where they were. He knew she shared a place in Hell's Kitchen with another struggling actress. Said her roommate was *a little psycho but in a fun, cute way.*

Mags also said her roommate was always staying with her boyfriend, some hedge fund dude with a sweet place that overlooked the park. Was that an informational signal? Letting him know they would have the place to themselves? Hank's palms sweat. Feels like his shoulders have climbed over his head. *Oh God, what the hell am I supposed to do?*

Mags kisses him.

Hank's shoulders ease back down. All his useless

fears melt away. Any stress he's been carrying around about Chef, his family, money, and what to do about every little this and that crap has simply gone the way of the dodo. This is a moment he wants to hold on to. Needs to cling to like a shelter in a storm.

Her lips so soft. How she smells. How she's holding him tight. Absent of fear. Absent of questions.

They take a small step back. Smiles wide. Eyes full of wonderful, funny feelings.

"You close Friday?" she asks in a sweet whisper.

"Yes. I do close." Hank has no idea what his schedule is, but he'll kill someone to change shifts if he has to. "I close Friday."

"Cool. Let's do some work on that bottle Friday."

Hank fights for cool. It's not there. No words coming.

"After we close," Mags helps him. "After we finish work Friday night."

"Yes. Of course. Done."

She breaks off a playful laugh. You couldn't knock the smile off Hank's face with a bat made of steel. Mags gives him another quick kiss with a longer, stronger hug, then turns, heading up the steps to her building's door.

Hank stands, feet planted in the concrete. Before opening the door, she turns back, giving him a wave

TABLE 13   49

goodnight. He waves back, hoping the look on his face isn't as goofy as he thinks it is. He waits to make sure she gets into the building safely. Not sure what he'd do if something did happen, but he'd like to think he'd do something somewhat brave.

Shoving his hands down into his pockets, he makes his way down the street.

He's got a place that overlooks the park too. Not his, of course. Sure, his trust fund, douchebag, rock band cousin lets him stay there, but he could have played that card. Needs to tuck that away. That's maybe something cool he can work with. Dammit. What was he thinking? Why didn't he...

No. No, you did good, he tells himself.

The events of the night run rip-riot through his head. All the moments. Almost begging to find something wrong with it.

Stop it, dumbass.

He balls up his fists inside his coat pockets, then breathes out. Forces himself to admit it was a great night. Begs his mind to accept the greatness of what's happened tonight. Didn't realize he was smiling until he felt the fatigue in his cheeks.

His phone buzzes. There's a text from his mom.

Hope to talk soon. Hope you're doing well.

"Shit."

Shoulders creep back up. Guilt flooding in. Feels

like Captain Reality has something to add to this evening. The real world is back. It allowed him a quick, feel-good break, but it always comes back— and the real world always wants its pound of Hank.

Fists clench tighter. Pulse ticks up. Thoughts roar, then land on a single image. Mags's face. A frozen grin. Eyes lit up with life. He tries to hold on to the image of her. A wonderful painting hung in the living room of his mind. Soaks in the vision of her.

Mom's face pops back with the buzz of another text.

Don't worry about calling if you're busy.

She'll call soon.

Hank tries to picture his father's face. Maybe his broken brain has healed enough to see what he's failed to see. He stops in the middle of sidewalk. Two men almost knock him over as Hank squeezes his eyes closed. Searching deeper and deeper into the troubled hallways of his mind. His thoughts rifle through pictures of men he's met who look like other people's fathers. Snapshot of dads from TV and movies. Commercial dads pushing breakfast crap, sensible cars, and chewable vitamins.

But not him. Not the man who provided the sperm to the equation. The man who was supposed to love him. Love his mom. He simply can't see him.

TABLE 13   51

Blocked. Not allowed. Not a single frame of his damn father's face.

"Shit." He opens his eyes, tears forming along the edges. Wiping them clear, he thumb-taps a call to his mom.

"Hey." His voice cracks as he takes a right down 52nd. "Hey, Mom. How's it going?"

PART TWO

SEVEN
NOW

THERE'S A RAPID-FIRE, *machine gun beat to his heart.*

Body and mind are still reeling from the car crash moments ago.

Stumbling through the thick night, desperate for something that resembles salvation, he dares to hope. Foolish as it seems, it's the first time in a long time, and it feels good.

Won't last, but Hank burns it up like fuel.

The dim light from the house in the distance carves a path for him in the dark. A pinhole of hope to cling to. His brain itches. Legs burn. He forces himself to keep pushing toward it. Shoves down his fear. Swats away the icy fingers that claw and dig into his mind ever since that night.

The night everything changed.

As his head thumps and throbs, he scrambles to return to that hope rather than what's happened to him. Maybe this house with the light is the safety he's hoping for.

Maybe it's a fresh house of horrors.

The spinning dizziness is coming on strong. A subtle reminder of how much blood he lost during the crash. During the fight before it. The pain is getting worse. An empty sensation like his life is flowing away from him. He hears his mom's voice inside his head.

Keep moving, Hank. You changed their plan. Altered their environment. Don't you dare stop because they will never even think about quitting.

"I won't," Hank mumbles through his busted mouth. "Keep moving, man."

He stumbles. His body flings forward. He seems to hang in the air, then his palms slam down hard onto rough weathered wood. The spinning in his head is a full-on cyclone. White globs form along the outer edges of the spins. His feet flop, hanging just above the ground.

He was so lost in his own damn mind that he tripped, stumbling on the front steps of the porch. His world rocks and slides as if he's trapped in an earthquake while standing underwater. His body moves in

TABLE 13   57

slow motion. Limbs won't respond to his mind's commands.

Get up! his mom screams inside his head. *They will never, ever stop.*

With everything he has left, Hank shoves himself up off the deck. A gust of cool wind almost knocks him back down. He steadies himself by gripping a rickety column made of raw wood. Works to find his breathing. Tries to establish a stable center point for his bouncing vision. He has to go inside. One way or another.

He knocks on the door.

Waits. Not sure if he wants someone to answer or not. Hank is all but drained dry of strength. Muscles are heavy and uncooperative.

He knocks again. Wants someone to open the door or not be there at all. Desperate for an answer to the question—is someone home? He hears nothing. He knocks again, louder this time, but still nothing from inside the house. He can't wait any longer. Sucking in a deep breath, he pushes against the door with his shoulder turning the knob as quietly as he can.

It opens.

There's a warm glow inside, lighting what looks like a living room. Homey furnishings. Quilts and family pictures on the wall. The bouncing hum of jazz plays in the background. Miles Davis Hank thinks it might be. He remembers Mags liking Miles Davis when his stuff plays at the restaurant sometimes. There is a wonderful smell of home cooking that fills the air.

This place looks like somewhere you would want to stay on a family vacation. Well kept. Clean. Safe. Hank pushes it all down. Hope can only make him sloppy. Trust nothing. But he knows he knows he has no choice but to trust this house. If he finds hope and trust here, then maybe, just maybe, he might make it through this.

Something that seemed impossible.

Hank places one foot inside. Fights the spins. Holds on to what he can, taking each step slow and easy. He takes in everything about the home with a mixture of wonder, relief, and fear. His shoulders come down, but his stomach twists in knots.

A voice calls out. It's coming from the kitchen.

Hank stops. Wants to become a hole in the universe. Whoever this is can't be worse than what's out there. Right? Not possible. Whoever lives here has no idea what's out there roaming in the dark.

Hank's legs give out, the crash is taking its toll. Dropping down to one knee, he tries to hold himself up by grabbing a chair. His hands give up before his mind does. Hank slips down to the floor. He grabs his head, struggling to hang on to his slipping conscious-

TABLE 13   59

ness. The white globs are winning. They'll overtake his vision in no time.

A man's voice speaks. Closer now.

Craning his neck, Hank sees an elderly man shuffling out from the kitchen, wiping his hands on a dish towel. A confused look is plastered on his wrinkled, bulldog face.

He says something, but Hank can't understand a word he's saying. A mumbled salad of verbs and adjectives spoken in a foreign tongue through a wet sock. Hank is all but gone. Everything that he is or will ever be is slipping away. Hope is all he has left. Hope he's reached that elusive safe place.

He manages a single word.

"Help."

Everything goes blinding white before it goes dark.

EIGHT
THEN

FRIDAY NIGHT. The restaurant is roaring.

Blurs of staff move and weave while serving the elite and those who want to feel elite for an evening. Toothy fake smiles flash between them all. Moments of polite behavior blend effortlessly with condescension and disdain. The dance of the service industry is performed here six days a week, noon to ten.

The love/hate smell of steak fills Hank's lungs. He's coming in hot tonight. Moving with purpose. Needs to clock in. He pauses, smiles big, and keeps his hands behind his back as guests pass by. All of them in clothes worth more than his father's funeral.

Hank checks his tie. He's running so damn late, but he doesn't care. He was on the phone with his mom again this afternoon and lost track of time. It was the right thing to do. Mom is not doing well even

TABLE 13   61

though she'd never say it. Hank hates the lost feeling of not knowing what to do. Mom wanted him to come here. *Go to New York and slay the dragon,* she said with a mad flash in her eyes.

Last night and again today, Hank brought up the idea of him coming home. His mom told him he was being silly. Told him to stay in New York and do good, but Hank could hear it in her voice. His mom is too old, too broken to shoulder everything back home.

Hank looked at flights. He can get to Texas maybe next weekend. Not cheap, but not too insane. Right now, though, he needs to get through this shift—hopes it's a good one—and then beg Chef for a weekend off. The first step is to check his uniform.

Hank steps quick toward the restroom.

Adjusting his belt, he lines it up so it is perfectly centered with his tie. Smoothing out an unruly eyebrow, he performs a final appearance check in the mirror before he walks the floor. He realizes tonight's check-in is a little more than simply something to appease the gods of the house. This pre-shift mirror time is more than the usual last look so Hank's appearance gives Chef Psycho one less thing to bust his balls about.

No. Tonight's final check-in is making sure he's sorted before Mags puts her eyes on him.

He knows logically it makes no sense to worry about it. She's seen him. Many times. Not going to get more Thor-like standing here in the bathroom, no matter how straight his damn eyebrows are. There's a pang of guilt of even thinking so much about Mags when the situation at home is such shit.

Stop, he hears Mom say inside his head.

He's transported back home to when his father died. Hank sat beside him on the kitchen floor. This was his final time with him. Later, his mom would place her soft hand on his shoulder and tell him, *Your life is yours.* Her voice was weak and strained, but there was strength flexing beneath it. *He's lived his life. Did with it what he pleased, made his choices.* She turned him around, tears streaming down the strongest face he'll ever know. *Now I need you to go and do likewise. Just do it better. Live a magical life, Henry.*

Hank smooths out his eyebrow once more. Wipes a growing tear away before it fully forms.

Although the sentiment is wonderful and seared into his memory, it is hard to parse out his mom's words. *Slay the dragon* and *magical life* are awesome, and they've pulled Hank along so many times since he came to New York, but it is a funny mix of images rattling around one's head. Dragon slaying comes from a book she read him when he was little. One they both loved. Can't help but laugh a little as he

TABLE 13   63

decides to stop fighting back the tears. Just lets them roll.

Looking at himself, he cycles through the labels. Small-town boy. Failed writer. Waiter. His Mom's son. He catches a tear before it hits his perfect, shift-ready shirt. Smiles as he squeezes it in his hand.

"Slay the dragon," he whispers.

Such an odd yet perfect moment.

Hank hopes Mom somehow knows she's always in his thoughts. Has to believe that having a drink with Mags is the *magical life* Mom was talking about. He can picture her saying it to him. Can hear her say the words. Mom's voice warm and wonderful, with all her strength and kindness.

Then he tries to see his father's face. He can see his hand holding his. His body is on the kitchen floor. But his face... He can't. It's only a blur. Sometimes it swirls. Sometimes it doesn't. It drives Hank crazy. He has no pictures of him. Mom quietly took them. Hank has memories of him, but his broken brain will not allow him to see his father's face. Another thought stops him cold, spinning his head in a better direction than his father. His mind has found some unearthed anxiety to slam on the breaks at this moment.

What if Eat the Rich isn't working tonight? How will we get that bottle?

He feels his mom shake her head at him with that

sly smile she gave him when he was a kid. The same sly smile she gave him when Hank freaked out before leaving home to come to New York. She told him to put that big brain on hold and let the world turn.

That big brain decides asking himself the questions again is important.

What if Eat the Rich is working tonight? How will we get that bottle?

"Who cares? You'll figure it out." Gives his face a soft slap. "Idiot."

A toilet flushes. Hank's spine stretches long and straight like a tree. He was so lost inside his own head he didn't think to check if he was alone.

Dammit.

Out from the stall walks Chef. Bubbling psycho eyeing Hank as he walks toward him. A man about to squash a bug. Hank's heartbeat ticks up as Chef moves to the sink. He holds his hands up and out in front of him as if he were a surgeon.

No eye contact as he uses his elbows to work the old-school hot and cold knobs. Long, chrome handles extended out, made to look new and slick with a bit of the past. The owner—meaning investor—hated the finicky touchless faucets and specifically asked for the sinks to be *proper*.

"You like talking to yourself?" Chef asks. "Some bullshit princesses in a bullshit story telling them-

TABLE 13   65

selves pretty bullshit into the mirror to soften the hurt before they fail tonight. Again."

"Sorry. I thought I was the only one in here."

"Don't apologize. Children need to soothe themselves."

"Not what I'm doing, Chef."

"You..." He laughs then stops on a dime. Gets more soap. Elbows the water even hotter. The steam is fogging up the bottom of the mirror. "You yap-yapping away at your own face before you fuck up my floor. That's funny stuff." Bigger laugh. "Okay. Guess that works for some people."

"I'm going to get ready for the start of my shift. Thank you, Chef."

"Don't thank me." Elbows the water even hotter. "Just do better, like you said to me the other night. Or —I don't know—slay the dragon?" Chef laughs.

The words stab at Hank. No way Chef would know those words were his mom's. Sacred statements a mom told a son at a moment of trauma. Hank must have repeated them out loud without knowing it, too lost in his thoughts to realize it.

Hank sucks in a deep breath, releases it slow. Fighting to keep his cool.

It's not easy.

"I'll try, Chef."

"Try?"

"Yes."

"The last five tried too."

Everything in Hank wants to grab this guy—this fucking guy—by the neck, put his face in the scalding water pouring down the gooseneck faucet. Hold his thrashing body while he boils like a lobster in a pot. But he needs this job. Especially after talking with Mom. Needs to be the bigger person. Keep this job.

"Sorry. Thank you, Chef."

"Yeah?" Elbows the water off. "Just said don't apologize, and you sure as shit shouldn't thank me." Chef moves within an inch of Hank's face. "I give simple instructions. So simple people can understand. I offer an order to things. Details that stack on top of one another, and they matter more and more and fucking more—"

"Yes, Chef."

"You need to listen. Process. Make my words your words. And *do better* than your hillbilly past allows."

Hank's knuckles pop as his hands form fists.

"Yes, Ch—"

"I never wanted you. I told those money clowns not to hire you, but they liked your little folksy way of talking and how you were with the tables and blah-blah-fucking-blah."

Something clicks in Hank's head.

TABLE 13   67

"I'm a good worker, you asshole. I work fucking hard here."

Chef stops. Takes a step back. Cocks his head as if Hank had begun speaking in tongues. Puts one hand on his hip, eyes wide, his other hand pressed tight to his chest. Looks like a '50s housewife who's heard something that's pearl-grasping offensive.

"My stars," Chef says. "In all my days…"

"Okay. Look, Ch—"

"*Look*?"

"Sorry. I didn't mean to—"

"There's that unwanted apology again."

"I did not mean to—"

"To what?" Chef pushes in closer. Face red. Veins bulging. "Hillbilly Hank didn't mean to fucking do what?"

In Hank's periphery, there's movement. The steel door of the last stall is opening. Slow and quiet, lights bouncing off the polished metal as it opens.

Chef grabs Hank's face. Thumbs pressing into his cheeks. His fingers digging into the back of his head. Hank should be furious. Country Hank would put this guy into the wall, but he keeps his eyes on the movement from the back of the room.

Two people slip out from the stall.

Silent but fast. Quick bare feet.

Hank's eyes strain. He can make out shapes but

can't quite see who. He steals a look. His heart catches in his throat.

"Look at me." Chef's intensity cranks as he squeezes Hank's face harder. "All eyes on—"

There's a snap. Dull like rubber bands on skin.

Hands grab Chef as he starts to turn.

Hands covered in blue surgical gloves attack at blinding speed. Nathan's bare feet stomp down, planting in a wide stance on the bathroom tile. His shoulders square as he breathes out, lips forming an O. Not a single movement of muscle is wasted.

Nathan snaps Chef's neck.

NINE

THE MUTED CRACK vibrates through Hank.

His hands slap the cool sides of the sink, catching himself. Hanging on by his fingertips.

Gina glides in, bumping Hank aside before he can even process what's happening, and catches Chef's falling body as if she already knew which way he'd drop. A pro fielding a fly ball. Nathan and Gina are laser-focused. Intense yet calm. A raging storm contained that will not unleash until needed.

Nathan goes to the door. Leans against it holding it closed. Seemed to already know there was no way to lock it from the inside.

Hank wants to call out, tell them to stop, to fight them somehow, but something won't allow him to do anything. He can only stand motionless, staring at Nathan.

Nathan looks back at him, void of expression.

Hank thinks of his faceless father.

Gina wrestles Chef's lifeless body, turning his shoulders, holding the body with one shoulder pointing toward the floor and the other to the ceiling. With a grunt, using her thighs and popping triceps, she raises Chef's head and body above the sink. His dead weight is getting the best of her, but she fights through it. A shotgun blast of spit from her lips. Muscles coil under her skin. Veins plump along her neck.

"Please back up, Hank," she says through gnashed teeth, holding Chef steady.

Hank moves back. Nathan puts a calming hand on his shoulder, pulling Hank toward him. His touch chills Hank to the bone.

Gina looks at Nathan. Nathan gives a nod.

She lets go. Her arms held open wide as she takes a giant step back.

Chef's head crashes down, slamming into the hard edge of the sink. There's a crack of bone. Crunch of cartilage. His body slumps into a pile on the floor. A patch of blood on the sink marks the impact. Without hesitation, Gina turns on some water from the sink, cups her hands under it, then splashes it on the tile near Chef's feet.

Gina wipes her brow. Looks to Nathan. *There.*

TABLE 13   71

Done.

A scream forms inside Hank. A call for help that he snatches away before it explodes out into the air. They were so fast. The world changed in a blink.

Only now does he notice Gina's dress is unzipped, pulled halfway down. One breast half exposed. She slinks back toward the stall barefoot. Adjusting her dress, she slips on the black laced panties that are crumpled in a pile, then picks up her silver high heels from the floor.

Zip.

Hanks turns around. Nathan is adjusting his pants. Working his belt. Buttoning up his shirt. It's all happened so fast. Information is ripping along at the speed of light. Too much to process. Questions pop, bursting inside his racing mind.

Were they having sex in the bathroom?

Did they hear my argument with Chef? Heard what was going on, then decided to kill him?

What the—

"It's okay, Hank." Nathan keeps his voice low but layered with a strange warmth.

Gina moves, almost floating, like moving along a model's runway. Her face is bright, full of fun, with electric eyes. Heels back on. Dress has been addressed. As she reaches Hank, she spins, turning around so her back is facing him. Her long dark hair covers most of her exposed back. Toned hard muscle under soft skin. Tan. Perfect.

"Give it a zip-zip, Hank?"

Hank's mind rejects the idea of requesting his hands to help zip up this woman's dress. Complete muscle failure.

"Don't overthink it, darling." Her voice is like velvet sandpaper.

As Gina pulls her hair up, Hank looks closer. He sees tiny lines like cracks in a masterpiece. Raised and lighter than the rest of her perfect skin. Different lengths. Multiple angles.

Scars?

There's one that snakes down where her neck meets her body, then trails and fades as it reaches her shoulder blade. Hank's writer brain goes to work. The violence she's seen. The trauma she must have experienced. *Child abuse? Nathan abuse?* The locations make it impossible to be self-inflicted.

What the hell has this person been through?

Thinks of his mom.

"I did that one," Nathan whispers into Hank's ear, gently touching one of the scars. Speaking as if he's pointing out stars in the sky. "Oh, and that one… and that one."

Nathan helps Hank's hand find the zipper.

Gina giggles like a child.

TABLE 13   73

"Now." Nathan leans back, still pressing against the door. "We're all leaving now. Gina and I will exit out the front."

Gina spins back around, facing them.

"Gina, please wait out front under the canopy, if you wouldn't mind. While I meet dear Hank in the alley?" Gina nods. Hank's face hangs from his skull. He's gone out of body. "Hank, buddy, you need to stroll out the back. Move with some urgency but not like your tits are on fire. Don't run or look rushed. Say you need to take a call if anyone asks you anything."

"What?" Hank looks at Chef's body. Head spinning. "You… I can't just—"

"Can and will." Nathan thumbs toward Chef's lifeless body. "They'll find him. There are security cameras on the front door and the back. As well as the entrance to the bathrooms."

Hank's blood runs cold.

How does he know that? How do they know to move the way they move? What the hell is —

"So." Nathan places his hands on Hank's face—much like Chef did—then nods. "As you can plainly see, there's a real need to leave immediately."

"If not sooner," Gina adds.

"And do what I suggested?" A look to Gina.

"Always, darling."

"I didn't do anything," slips out from Hank.

"Doesn't matter." Nathan holds Hank's eyes a little too long. Makes an odd noise with his mouth and tongue. Something like a cluck, something Hank's never heard before. Gina makes the same strange noise. Nathan releases Hank's face. The impressions of his fingers linger.

Hank jumps off the rip-peel sound of rubber being pulled from skin.

Nathan and Gina free their hands from the blue surgical gloves. Hank catches the scent of latex and sweat. Nathan folds his gloves nice and neat, then hands them to Gina. Then she, as if on instinct, slips them into a ziplock bag, seals it—yellow and blue make green—then drops the bag inside her purse. Hank can't be sure, but he's almost certain he saw the bag slide over the handle of a small gun inside that tiny purse.

"I'm not going anywhere with you. This…" His shaking hand points at Chef's body. "You killed him."

"You're upset," Gina says.

"Understandable," Nathan says.

"True. Not helpful, annoying, and silly, but understandable."

"You're insane." Hank spins away, braces himself with both hands on the sink. "This isn't happening."

"Now," Nathan says, ignoring him, "I'm going to open this door and—"

TABLE 13   75

The door thumps. The knob turns.

Nathan's body jerks forward but pushes back hard on the door. He removes a knife from his jacket. The same *steak knife* Hank saw the other night.

Hank turns, about to call out, but Gina jams her hand over his mouth.

"Hang on, brother." Nathan talks to the door with his best southern accent. Grips the knife tight. "My buddy is sick as a damn dog in here. Be out di-rectly."

Gina leans in, lips centimeters from Hank's ear.

"Now or never." Her whisper is wrapped in sugar. "Don't make tonight worse. It's unnecessary. This can go peacefully or noticeably shittier."

Hank eyes the knife. Mind pops like popcorn.

Nathan's whole demeanor has changed. Gone is the playful Manhattan monument to premium blood-lines and wealth. His eyes are hard. Body stiff. Focused. A snake coiled, ready to strike. Nothing makes sense. Hank's entire world has flipped. He only knows one thing right now—these two will not hesitate to kill whoever's out there. Some unlucky guy who just wants to use the bathroom at the worst time possible.

Hank closes his eyes and then forces a nod.

"Super sweet. Super cool, Hank." Gina's words have an ugly smile.

Nathan pushes off the door but keeps a foot at the

bottom to hold it closed. Pocketing the knife, he wraps an arm around Hank's neck, pushing his head down and away from easy view. Giving the illusion he's helping a drunk buddy. Gina glides behind the door, hiding as it opens. Nathan is careful to block the view inside the bathroom.

"I'm really sorry. My boy here is so red wine fucked-up." Still working a thick southern accent. Turns his head avoiding direct eye contact. Always moving forward. "Sorry as hell."

Hank feels Nathan's fingers push his head down as he pulled along. Didn't get a look at the man at the door. Hears him mutter a question. Sounds like an older gentleman. Thick cologne. A hint of wealth and breeding in the man's tone and rhythm of speech. Hank has picked up on these things during his time working here.

"I wouldn't go in there, brother." Nathan moves along but not rushing. "I'm getting the manager. Need a biohazard crew to do some work in there. Try next door. Better bathroom anyway."

From the corner of Hank's eye, with his head pressed down, he can see the high-end sneaker-shoes of the older, wealthy gentleman pause, then move away from the bathroom.

"You're doing simply grand, Hank." Nathan's

TABLE 13   77

voice is labored but still calm and cool. "Almost done here."

Just as he thinks of struggling, Nathan releases him. Gentle shoves him toward the kitchen.

"Go out the back like we said. Meet you in the alley." Nathan's gaze is searing. "Everything is going to be cooler than cool."

Hank blinks. He could probably make a run for it. Plenty of people here. He can call the cops. He didn't do anything wrong.

"Hank?"

The sound of Mags's voice freezes his heart. Nathan stops. His head cocks birdlike.

No. No. No.

"You okay?"

Hank's eyes find focus. He spins around to Mags. She is standing off the edge of the main dining room. Staff and guests move around her like she's the eye of the storm.

"Work that wise, writer mind of yours, Hank." Nathan speaks low and clear into his ear, then also whips around to Mags. "Darling. I remember your lovely face from the other evening. Unfortunately, our Hank here is not well. I'm helping him to a clinic down the street."

Mags nods, looking to Hank for some form of confirmation.

An image of Nathan's knife pops into his mind. Sharp and shining bright. His fingers gripping it tight. The sound of Chef's neck snapping echoes in his ears. The crack of his head dropped to the sink. Crunch of bones. Limbs and torso slumping into a pile on the tile.

"She is pretty, Hank." Nathan's whisper is hard as he scans the room. "Pity if pretty had to get ugly."

"I'm okay." Hank's voice breaks. "Rain check?"

"Yeah, sure." Mags's face is wrapped in worry. She turns, looking back at the hostess stand that's stacking up and waiting for her return. "I've gotta go back—"

"That's okay. I'll call you later."

Mags nods before rushing back to her duties at the front of the restaurant. It was only for a flicker, but she held his eyes for a caring second. As if holding his hand with a look. Not nearly long enough.

Nathan shoos him along, flinging his wrist toward the kitchen doors.

Deep breath in, Hank pushes through, quick steps cutting through the kitchen. Keeping his head down, he rushes past the waitstaff, kitchen staff, and dishwashers. All of them move at double speed as the heart of the dinner rush is upon them.

Hank's drumming pulse pounds. He shoves away the urge to scream. There's a twist inside of him that's keeping him from grabbing someone and pleading

TABLE 13   79

for help. Thinks of Nathan standing in the dining room watching Mags. Knife within reach. A blink away from destroying an innocent, precious person.

Hank plants his palm on the exit, pushing through the door at the back of the kitchen that's used for deliveries. The night air hits his face. A pleasant slap of cool. It wraps around his body. A comforting moment of peace he may never know again.

Gina rounds the corner. Stops. Cocks her hip, then curls her fingers up and down in an odd *hello* before slinking toward him. Nathan stands behind him, nudging him forward toward her. Hank didn't even hear him coming or notice he was there.

Unable to cling to a single, stable thought, Hank's vision tilts. The words *this isn't real* run in a loop inside his head. Feels like he's falling, like the rug has been yanked out from under him. The world he knew, as imperfect as it was, is gone, has become new and unthinkable. Years undone in seconds.

"What do you want?" Hank asks.

"Immortality." Nathan coughs. Hard, almost choking.

"A never-ending good time with a side of happy," Gina adds, rubbing his back.

"I'm finding a cop. I didn't do anything." Hank turns. Makes it two steps.

"Hank, really? You're so much better than that

basic bitch sort of thinking," Gina calls out. Hank stops and turns back to her. Gina motions to the restaurant. "What would you say happened here? Exactly."

"If asked." Nathan wipes his mouth, recovering from his cough. "And only if asked."

"What I heard was an argument." Gina shrugs. "Sure, look, my man and I were doing a thing in the stall—naughty, naughty. Fortunately, we were wrapping up. But ya know, we could hear this brewing, raging tussle brewing between two gentle-bros. I'm certain the time stamp on the security footage will verify when everyone entered. And, of course, the recent semen inside of me will certainly verify our dirty, sexy truth."

"Please, what do you want? I don't have any money. I don't have any—"

"Look at you. Don't worry, buddy. You've got so, so much to give. Great value in you." Nathan extends his hand as if introducing the whole wide world to Hank. "Time you learn how to be the environment that alters the products."

A cold shiver rattles Hank.

Gina takes his trembling hand.

"Welcome to the first day of the rest of your life."

TEN

"DO YOU FIND FATE FUNNY?" Gina asks.

She is leading Hank by the hand into a jaw-dropping hotel suite. A space designed to induce stammering upon sight. A temporary playground for royalty and rock gods.

"I find fate kinda funny," she says.

The floor-to-ceiling glass shows off the most amazing view Hank has ever seen. The city is framed perfectly. An incredible living, breathing panoramic shot pulled straight from a movie. Hank half expects aliens and superheroes to go to war across the skyline in front of him.

Nathan and Gina move with purpose.

Gina shuts the door, locking every lock. Nathan grabs a laptop from a table and immediately starts to work the bottom with a power screwdriver. He removes the hard drive like a pro, then cracks the laptop over his knee, tossing the busted-up computer into a large black bag that Gina unzips and lays out on the floor seconds before the busted laptop lands.

A perfect machine in motion. No orders or instructions given. Both moving in sync, performing, executing a plan that's already been discussed, analyzed, agreed upon, and understood.

Gina unzips her dress, letting it fall to the floor. Sculpted and scarred, she steps out from the clump of tender fabric she wore like a second set of skin. A long, tall tattoo stretches along the side of her body. It runs from the top of her ribcage, ending slightly above her hip. She leaves her heels on, letting the click and clack provide some rhythm to the otherwise quiet room.

Hank squints, trying to get a good look at the tattoo. Trying to maybe understand.

It's a female devil. Long dark hair—like Gina's—with horns poking through and dressed in a tux while holding a cigarette, a serpent like tail twisting behind her.

Nathan tosses her the hard drive.

Hank takes a step toward the door. Nathan snaps his fingers, waves him into the room. Hank stops cold, then stumbles forward a few steps into the living room of the suite. Nathan puts up a hand

TABLE 13   83

instructing him to stop, then points down. He's being directed to a couch facing that window that overlooks the city. Hank takes a seat as if he's been scolded by an adult in charge.

His thoughts spin, blurring into streaks and smears of nonsense. Dancing eyes look out into the endless sea of lights, concrete, and steel that line the night. Thousands, millions of people out there who aren't trapped in an insane hotel paradise. He thinks of all of them watching TV, cleaning their homes, arguing about money, having sex for the first time, or the last, and all the other people out there living their lives without Nathan and Gina. Crazy to be jealous, but he is. He balls his fists tight.

This can't be happening. He must have hit his head, his brain drowning in knee-deep delusion. He's really in a hospital bed. Tubes and drugs working his body and mind. His mom by his bed. Mags will visit. Hold his hand.

Click, clack, click-clack.

Gina's heels sound off as she passes through the sprawling hotel suite. Nathan tosses another snapped laptop into the bag on the floor, then flips the hard drive with a flick of his wrist. Gina catches it one-handed with her right hand as she carries the other hard drive in her left.

She places the drives into a microwave in the

kitchen. Kicks off her high heels, landing them close to the bag of busted laptops. Nathan tosses her another hard drive. She puts it in the microwave along with the others, then tosses Hank a beer from the fridge.

Hank catches it on instinct rather than desire. No intention of drinking it. He wants to ask questions. Wants answers he knows he won't get. He wants to scream for help until his throat tears. Wants to run hard to the door. Escape or die trying.

"Nervous feelings?" Gina nods with under-standing eyes. "You have them, right?"

Hank stares back at her. Words stuck inside his mouth, unable to come out. Any form of clear thought falls like a mudslide. Squeezing his eyes closed, he holds on to an image of Mags. A single frame of her face, her eyes, everything about that night cuts into his memory. Their *sort of date*. Memories with razor-sharp claws digging deep but then releasing. Fluttering away, chased away, self-protection working overtime.

Hank's mind always seems to come back around to defend itself. Hurts too much to think about her. *Is she worried about me? Will she just find someone new? Of course she will. I was soooo far out of my depth.* These scary mental wounds are already beginning to close as his thoughts drift away from her, away from the

TABLE 13   85

good. Scarring over in order to protect the greater good.

He does this.

He thinks about how his mom used to worry so much. He thinks of his father not caring about anything. Father's swirling faceless body towering over him. Over Mom.

"Fair enough." Gina pats him on the knee. "We'll cue the topic up later."

Gina picks up her shoes by the straps, glides back to the kitchen, taps at the microwave, leaving the hard drives to pop, crack, and cook behind her. Sparks light up the darkened kitchen like fireworks going off in a small aquarium. She picks up her dress from the floor then drops it, along with her shoes, into the bag that Nathan dumped the laptops.

As Gina slips off, she turns back, giving Hank a soul-melting glance with a curl of her lip just before disappearing into a dark bedroom. Nathan removes his suit, dropping each piece into the bag. Jacket. Shirt. Belt. Until he's stripped down to his designer underwear.

He's a specimen. Carved from stone, matching the toned, sculpted body of Gina. Not a bodybuilder with swollen muscle mass. He's sleek. Designed for move-ment. More Olympic swimmer than beefy action hero. Has a collection of scars as well.

Hank's eyes are drawn to something.

Much like Gina, there is a devil tattoo running from the top of Nathan's ribs down to just above his hip. A male devil with a serpent-like tail in a tux smoking a cigarette. There is one clear difference between Nathan's and Gina's bodies, other than the obvious. He has circular disks stuck to his skin—two that Hank can see. Nathan checks, inspects them, then picks up his phone.

Hank looks harder. They seem to serve a purpose. Nathan taps at the screen of his phone, then looks at one of them on his forearm. They aren't random. At least they don't look that way. It looks like some have been carefully placed along his spine.

Not patches slapped or stuck on. They are made of something like thin, hard plastic. Smooth and clean. Hank remembers Nathan coughing while they were in the street. Hard choking coughs. *Are they medical?*

"Look away," Nathan barks.

"What? Sorry, I—"

"Look away." Softer, asking.

Hank turns around so he's facing the window. Pointless because Hank can see everything through the reflection in the window's glass. Nathan probably knew this, as he yanks down his underwear, turning

TABLE 13   87

left and right, taking a moment to admire himself in the reflection before he leaves the room.

Gina returns, passing Nathan as he enters the bedroom. She's dressed head to toe in matte black with a thin backpack strapped to her back. Looks like something an advanced police or military unit would wear. Textured, tight, black tactical gloves cover her hands. Her hair is in a buzz cut. A mix of special forces and punk rock. She pulls a tight skullcap over what's left of her hair. Hank blinks. No way she shaved her head in the brief time she left the room.

What the hell?

She stops, pausing to take in Hank's question mark expression. She drops a brunette wig into the bag and then bounces her eyebrows as her lip does that curl again.

"This is all pretty bonkers, right?" she asks as she removes a pack of Clorox wipes from the backpack, immediately going to work on the doorknobs and anything else she can find. "It's okay if you think so. I think so too, from time to time."

Hank doesn't know if he's supposed to respond, let alone what he should say.

"We're not going to hurt you." She's back into the kitchen area. Checks the microwave. Nods in approval after looking over the nuked hard drives.

Starts wiping down the handles on the Subzero fridge. "Hurting you was not part of the plan."

The word *was* stabs like a spear.

"Is there a plan?"

"There is." She stops. Her stare bores through him. There's an unmistakable shift in her. "Of course there's a plan, silly man. What do you think?" Anger bubbles under her skin. She slams the wipes down on the counter. "You—what?—you think we don't think? That we're idiots? Random whackos? Is that what you think of me and my man?"

"I didn't—"

"Is it? That really what you think of us?" She stalks toward him, voice rising. "Tell me, Hank."

Hank shakes his head. Terror rockets. The speed, the velocity of the change in her is staggering. Her face has grown red, eyes almost popping out from her skull. She's not letting this go, not even close.

"Tell me, you piece of shit product of a boy." Screaming now. Spit flying. "Is that what you fucking think of us?"

"I'm sorry. I—"

"We control your world. You bend to what we create. And you think there's no plan? So, I'll ask one last time—Is. That. What. You. Think?"

"Gina." Nathan moves in fast with a bundle of

TABLE 13   89

sheets and bedding under his arm. "He does not think that. He wouldn't. Would you, Hank?"

"No." Hank clears his throat. "Of course not. No."

Gina smiles. Face returns to its normal shade.

Complete flip in her state of mind. Like a string was pulled inside of her. She kisses the top of Hank's head, then spins back around, returning to wiping down the hotel suite.

Hank's lungs start to work again. His heartbeat levels off.

Nathan stuffs wads of towels along with the bedding into the bag on the floor. He's dressed in the same fashion as Gina. All black, gloves, skullcap, with a backpack. Stopping, starting, constantly looking around, as if he's checking things off in his mind, but never frantic or showing a loss of control. Seemingly satisfied, he looks back to Gina. She's standing near the front door, scanning the room like she's checking off the same mental list. A system of checks and balances between them.

"Our friend Hank over there." Gina pushes her chin toward the couch "He was asking about the plan."

"Was he now?"

"Was indeed."

"You tell him the plan?" Nathan asks with a smile in his voice.

Hank watches the ping-pong conversation playing over the madness of the moment.

"Told him there was one," Gina says. "Do you have the tip for housecleaning?"

Nathan pulls out a wad of cash, tossing it onto the table. Much like what he gave Eat the Rich the other night. A lifetime ago.

"Not sure they'll find it, but we left it," Nathan says.

"It's the thought," Gina adds.

Hank tries to understand all that's happened. He's spinning. Worst-case scenarios blast like a cannon. His teeth grind. He knows he needs to find some calm, no matter how pointless that seems. Not sure calm will ever be part of his life, but he knows this rambling, out-of-control state of mind he's experiencing right now will not help him.

Think, Hank. His mom's words echo and fade.

He sees her face as they stand over his father. As she pulled him away from his body and brought him in close to her. Protecting him from it all.

Zip.

Nathan zips up the bag on the floor. The harmless sound makes Hank want to come undone. He didn't notice it before, but it has wheels on the bottom. Handle on the top. Looks like a bag used to travel with golf clubs, maybe, or a shortboard surfboard.

TABLE 13   91

"Ready?" Nathan asks.

Gina slips the Clorox wipes she's used to wipe down the suite into the same ziplock bag she used to discard the blue latex gloves in the restaurant bathroom.

Hank sits still like a statue. Eyes wide and vacant. A shell of what he was less than an hour ago. Repeats his internal command. *Think.*

Gina sits next to him on the couch. Places her hand on his knee.

Bumps rise across Hank's skin like an army.

"Hey. We need to go. As freaky as this may be, none of that really matters. Not one bit." She moves her hand up, only an inch, but still up his thigh. "While we sit here in the lap of luxury, the police are finding a dead cook in the little boys' room of the place where you used to work. They're asking questions, digging through security footage." Hank turns, locking eyes into hers. She nods, moving her hand up his thigh ever so slightly. "Maybe we did a good job with our exit, maybe we didn't, but either way, we—"

"*We?*"

"But either way"—Gina ignores his question, raising her free hand making a point—"no matter what's happening at that wonderful eatery, or what's going on in your pretty head, or in your precious little heart, we need to leave this fancy room. And yes, we do have a plan. And you're a big part of it. Do you believe me?"

Hank's mouth is bone-dry. Calm is failing him.

"Trust is key here, Hank. Signal that you believe."

Fighting them is useless. For now, at least. He must pick his moment. First, however, he needs to live long enough to have any moments to choose from.

He manages a nod.

"Good. Really good because you should believe in us. In our plan." Her hand grazes his crotch ever so slightly as she raises a finger, running it over his lips. Eyes wild and wide. "So happy we found you."

Before Hank can comprehend her words or the crazed, floating look in her eyes, she drops something into his lap. Picking it up, he realizes it's a black ski mask. Thin but padded. Soft but textured.

"It's time." Nathan claps his hands. "Wheels up."

Gina springs up from the couch, humming a tune. Hank peels away from the here and now as her murmured melody hums behind him. It's familiar, but he can't place it. A well-known song but the title escapes him. Something from the '70s, maybe the 80s. An earworm that plays with your head until you remember it or your mind snaps in two.

"Hank."

Gina's voice shakes Hank loose from the tune. He

TABLE 13   93

looks to them. Nathan and Gina stand side by side. Same ski masks pulled down over their faces.

"Now." Gina curls her finger, signaling it is time to join them. "Let's get started."

Nathan taps the screen of his phone. Gina smiles. She counts out loud. A countdown.

"Three…

"Two…

"One."

The lights go out.

ELEVEN

"IT'S COOL, HANK," Nathan says.

"Be cool," Gina adds.

The hotel suite is dark save for the lights of the city through the window. Provides some visibility but not much. Hank can make out the two of them standing still in the doorway.

This was expected. Part of whatever *the plan* is.

He feels Gina's hand grab his wrist, pulling him up off the couch and out through the door. His legs feel like concrete. Gina guides him, following Nathan down the dimly lit hotel hallway. Tiny lights run along the bottom of the walls just above the floor. This in case of emergency, backup lighting is designed to lead guests to some form of safety if need be. They have no idea what's roaming the hall right now.

TABLE 13   95

Aside from the sound of his thumping heart in his ears, he doesn't hear any other noises. No sounds coming from the rooms.

Nobody is peeking out into the hallway. No heads poking out, looking around, checking on the lights. No aggravated yells or shouts demanding for the lights to come on.

Nothing.

Hank has lost all track of time, but there's a chance some of the guests are either out on the town or asleep. Nathan moves in a quick jog, fast but quiet, stopping at a room about four doors down from the room they left.

Looking back, Hank sees the door to their room is wide open. There's a flicker that reflects off a framed picture hanging on the wall across from the door. Like a TV was left on. Hank squints hard to make out what he's seeing. A faint smell drifts into the hallway.

Like something is burning.

Another flicker. Then another. Then there's a flame. A tongue made of fire licks out from the door. He blinks. Looks again. There are the beginnings of fire inside the room.

"What the hell?" slips from Hank's mouth before he knew he said anything.

He pieces together that the long bag on the floor was not for transporting. It was a burn bag.

Gina yanks his hand down hard, demanding his focus. Looking ahead, he can see Nathan touching the door of another room. Running his hands over it. Inspecting it.

He turns back to Gina. She nods, pulling a knife.

Nathan kicks the door in.

Gina shoves Hank, forcing him inside as she rushes past him. Hank stumbles but finds his footing. The door behind him is left open. A warm rush of hope floods his chest. This is his chance. Now or never. He turns quick toward to the door, toward his escape. For a fraction of a second, he lets hope creep in. They made a mistake. They left him alone with a clear exit. They lost focus and—

Two strong hands slam him down to the floor.

His head snaps back as he lunges forward. Teeth rattle. Hank tumbles down hard on the tile, flips, rolls before stopping and ending up on his back, staring at the darkened ceiling. A rug stopped his roll. Even through the mask, he can smell the flowery cleaning products used on the rug.

Everything is a dark blur, cut here and there by the flickering light from the hall. Hank's eyes struggle to adjust, but he can tell that flickering from the hall is growing fast. Shadows of flames dancing. Smells of smoke gathering in the hallway. Hank pushes himself up to his knees.

TABLE 13   97

There's a confused voice of a woman from another room.

Maybe from the bedroom. Hank can only assume this layout is similar, if not identical to the room they were in. The woman screams. But only for a fraction of a second. There's a sound. Quick and sick. Sound of flesh being slashed. Hank feels the floor thump.

A man's voice booms. Barking, commanding, yet soaked in terror.

Multiple, lightning-fast, thick sounds end his voice. Changing, morphing it into a gurgle followed by another thud to the floor.

Hank can't breathe. He didn't see anything. Didn't need to.

The unmistakable hum of violence that traveled out from that dark room will never leave him. He tries to rationalize. His hyper-creative writer brain scrambling for other explanations, but there's no mistaking what has happened. They killed two people in this room in the coldest of blood.

Soft footsteps patter his way. Shadowy outlines of his captors closing in on him. Whipping his head around, back toward the door, he thinks of making another try for it.

I can make it.

But what if I don't?

The fire alarm wails. Strobes of light burst in the

hallway. Now he hears movement. Rising chatter from the other rooms on the floor. Shadows moving, bouncing in the hall. Hank feels hands pick him up off the floor. Lifting him up from under his arms, dragging, pulling him along.

"Got you, buddy," Nathan grunts.

They move fast away from the room. To the left, the fire has grown. Nathan takes a knife from Gina and tosses it underhanded into the fire.

"We're going to the stairs." Gina's mouth is an inch from Hank's ear, then she pulls back. "Fire! Go! Go!" Screaming out to the panicked hotel guests racing toward a door at the end of the hall. Back to Hank's ear. "We'll mix in with the crowd, then remove your mask and hand it to me. Got that?"

Feels like Hank's feet haven't touched the ground in hours.

Walking on air.

He thinks of walking with Mags. Thinks about the date he was supposed to have with her tonight. One he may never have.

"Do you understand?" Harder. Louder.

He nods. He feels Nathan place a hand on his shoulder. Gives it a squeeze as if he's trying to help a friend through a tough time.

"No," Hank says.

"Come again?" Nathan asks.

TABLE 13   99

"This is insane."

"What?" Gina asks.

Hank feels a click in his head. He shoves Nathan away, then pushes off Gina. Slipping from their grip just enough to break free. He slams his shoulder into Nathan as he tries to come back at Hank. The hit pushes him back an inch or two, turning his body, buying Hank a second. Hank shoves past them, running with all he has. Legs churn. Lungs choke on the smoke. He's running headlong toward the fire.

His feet skid to a stop.

The fire has overtaken the hall. Climbing up the walls in waves, meeting in an ocean of flames fully formed on the ceiling above. The heat is relentless, as if he's drifted too close to the sun. He watches the hotel door they left moments ago burn. All the death swallowed up by cleansing fire. In the room—the one with the clothes, the gloves they used from the restaurant, what's left of the laptops and hard drives—all the evidence has long since burned into a crisp pile of nothing.

A false hope rockets through Hank. Hope that Nathan and Gina have moved on, given up on the nice waiter from a small town in Texas, and will leave him alone as they mix in the crowd on the stairs.

A hand grabs his shoulder, spinning him around like a barstool.

A fist lands. Once then twice. His face cracks. Then a thundering punch to his gut doubles him over. White blobs form. The taste of his own blood rolls down his throat as he gags, trying to breathe. His legs wilt under him. The white globs are taking over.

"It's okay to be upset," Nathan says.

"Super okay," Gina agrees.

They stand on either side of him with his arms over their shoulders. Carrying him like a wounded soldier toward the stairs.

"But we do need you, Hank," Nathan says.

"Facts," Gina adds. "Ain't a plan without Hank. Is it now?"

Hank's entire world stops. Fire crackles behind him. His vision wipes it all into a stark white smear, holds it for a flutter of a wasp's wings before everything is swallowed by the dark.

TWELVE
NOW

HANK IS *awake and not awake at all.*

Stuck in a strange yet wonderful middle ground some-where between sleep and the terror of being awake. A limbo of gooey calm. Unstable fear potentially lurking outside his eyelids. Mixed yet separated, still grounded to this earth while not at all.

Thoughts flow thick like cold maple syrup.

He thinks he's lifting up his head and feels the strain in his neck, but he's not completely sure if that's happening at all. Seems like he is lifting his arms up in the air too. At the same time, he feels like he's lying completely coffin-still.

Is he imagining doing these simple things? Is he even alive at all?

Where is he? Is he here—meaning the last "here"

he remembers, the house with the light in the dark woods—or somewhere unknown?

That thorny word "here" is a tricky one to handle. He remembers the car crashing into the tree. The soul-jolting force. Time slowed to a crawl. Then the running—so much running—and stumbling through the woods. The dizziness from the blood leaving his body.

Finding and entering the house. The elderly man.

Foggy, messy noises, clogged earlike, but he thinks he might be hearing people. He's heard them before. Blotches of sound. Sprays of murmurs in the distance. Maybe that was a few minutes ago. Or was it days ago? A few seconds? Hard to grasp. Impossible to place. Someone is out there, but he can't confirm who it is or what is being said.

The words spoken seem like they are from the older man. The pattern and the tone feel like they are from the kind-faced elderly man who walked out from the kitchen after Hank stormed into his home. He caught a quick glimpse of him right before the world went black. It looked like he was cooking. No, he was doing the dishes...maybe. Seemed as if Hank had interrupted him from preparing his dinner or cleaning up shortly thereafter.

His fingers twitch. Some feeling returning.

At least Hank now knows he is lying on his back.

TABLE 13   103

That cannot be argued. Knows he's lying on something soft, like either a couch or a bed. Can feel it with the tips of his fingers. The sense of touch comes and goes along with everything else.

Again, he is neither asleep nor awake. He is simply here.

Whatever that means.

Wait. He can clearly hear the old man talking. That's him. No question. Still cannot make out the words, but Hank hears a conversation. A conversation between the old man and someone else. Another voice that counters the aging vocal cords of the kind-faced, dinner-dish man. A new voice, female, that is soft and calm. Low and serious at the same time.

Maybe they're arguing, maybe they're not. Really hard to say.

Hank tries to crack open his eyes. They refuse the request. Feels as if they are melted shut. His head pounds in a dull thump that matches his heartbeat. Not the sharp pain like before. Thoughts fade and return. Feelings slip and peel away. Time seems pointless. A raft floating in the middle of a giant ocean. No land for days. Powerless to change anything.

It feels like his body is being lifted.

As if he's being moved. Maybe even dragged. There's some pressure on the back of his heels, a lift under his shoulders. He must be being moved to another room. Maybe that's what that conversation was about. A chat about what to do with little old Hank Quinn.

Who the hell knows?

Even in this state of nothingness, he still smells that wonderful home cooking. If he could form a sentence, the subject of that sentence would be dinner. He should be afraid of everything, but fear isn't there. A frozen world wrapped in a velvet blanket that thaws and refreezes constantly. Easy to describe but impossible to define.

The sensation of being moved has stopped.

The sounds have stopped as well. Not only the voices of the old man and his female friend but all sounds. They've been replaced by a hum inside his mind.

Then one sound breaks the hum. Chopping through like a machete.

This one sound is clear. Nearby. It's the stretching, pulling, ripping of something. Of tape, maybe. Tape is being ripped away from a roll, pulled away from its spool.

Then he feels physical contact. This is a first. Unsolicited and not necessarily wanted, either.

On his arm, there's pressure. Then his head. A cold shiver rolls from the top of his skull down to his

TABLE 13   105

toes. There is moisture. What feels like a wet cloth is being applied to his skin, then more tape rips. Something soft and textured pressing on his flesh.

He imagines the old man and his wife bandaging him. Nursing his wounds. Caring for him.

He thinks of his mom. Of Mags as she smiles.

The hurt of hope sticks like a hypodermic needle. His mind runs, escaping back into the dark. Where it belongs. Hiding from everything that happened.

Chef's death. The hotel fire and murders.

What happened at the top of that parking garage in New Jersey.

THIRTEEN
THEN

THE SUNLIGHT IS CRUSHING.

Hurts to crack open one eye, let alone the two Hank would prefer for clear sight. His head pounds. Face throbs. His mouth is dry, coated with a paste he'd rather not identify. Can smell smoke from the hotel even though he knows he is not there anymore.

His body sways left and right and bounces. He's moving, but not sure where he is or where he's going. Hopes it's a hospital. A police station. His cousin's condo with Spartacus. Back home to his tiny hometown. Anywhere but where he's been.

Shit, he needs to feed Spartacus. After he gets cleaned up and gets his head right, he'll run back to the condo and feed him.

Wait.

Hank's stomach falls. Only takes a fraction of

TABLE 13   107

second to remember what happened. Remember that the idea of going anywhere is delusional.

Images pop. Sounds. Flashes of violence. Fire.

The restaurant bathroom. The hotel rooms. The bone-chilling sounds in the dark. Being shoved through the smoke-filled hallway. Fists pounding his face. He winces as he touches his nose. Tender as hell, but he'll live. He can't see himself, but he feels the soft padding of the bandage.

He's been taken care of.

His sight comes back little by little. The fog drifts as seconds pass. He's in the back seat of a car. More like a large SUV. A nice one at that. Plush, cool-to-the-touch leather. Air vents push even cooler, refreshing air across his face. The music is merely unattached sounds at first. A jumbled, tangled mess of notes and muddled words. As his head clears, he recognizes the tune. "Angel of the Morning" is playing clear as day.

He hears Gina hum along. She was humming the same tune in the hotel suite. The back of Nathan's head sways ever so slightly with the rhythm. The hope this was all some sort of fever dream is snuffed out.

Hank tilts his head. Grits his teeth. Hurts like hell.

He's lying down across the back of the SUV, dressed in different clothes than he remembers wearing. The tactical ski mask and gloves are gone. His carefully curated waiter uniform is gone as well. He's wearing a ridiculously soft navy-blue T-shirt, soft jeans, and bright white Nike Air Force 1 sneakers. A look he's seen many ultra-hip, ultra-cool New Yorkers wear into the restaurant. He had seen his favorite author—his author crush, Walter Scott—wear similar garb on countless interviews and bookstore events.

For months, Hank more or less stalked world-famous writer Walter Scott when he first moved to New York. Went to all his events. He's one of the reasons Hank even looked at the restaurant. He knew Mr. Walter Scott frequented the place with his latest, and probably soon-to-be former wife. Hank brought him water one time. He could barely speak, and what he did say was tragic garbage.

He should have said something vaguely coherent. Maybe something funny or a thing that would pass as interesting. A new thought sends a shudder through his body. He may never get a chance to. His mind returns to its racing. Remembering. His brain finding its footing. He's trapped. Held captive.

Wait.

Why did they dress me like Walter Scott? How would they know?

More important questions plume.

What do they want? Why won't they let me go?

TABLE 13   109

They haven't killed him. That's something positive, maybe, but what is their plan?

Don't ask, Hank. Gina lost her shit last time you asked about a plan.

"Think there's some water back there," Gina says. "If you'd like some."

Two bottles of water sit in the cup holders in front of him. They look nice, with cold beads running down the sides. He imagines opening both, dumping them over his throbbing head like a bottled water waterfall.

"Ibuprofen too," she adds. "But wait an hour or so. We gave you some this morning. That's hard on your liver, right? Kidneys"?

"Very hard." Nathan turns down the music.

"Where are we?" Hank coughs. Didn't realize how dry his throat was until he spoke.

"Not important," Nathan says.

"Not really material." Gina cracks open a water, handing it to Hank. "What's important, what's always important, is where are we going?"

"Okay. Fine." Hank gulps the water. "Where are we going?"

"Not important," Nathan says, turning the wheel.

Hank fights not to roll into the floorboard. The contents of his head slosh.

"He's right. Not really material either," Gina

agrees. "Got some stops to make. Then we can get started."

Hank freezes on the words *get started*.

"It's not perfect, but we'll make it perfect," Gina says. "Whatever you need."

"Your work is what's important. How's that sound, Hank?" Nathan asks. Coughs hard—a jolting whole body cough. Can barely get through his words. "That's what's important."

"I don't understand."

"Of course you don't, silly man. How could you?" Gina rubs Nathan's back. "Do you like your clothes? I found pics online of that guy. Ya know, that writer guy you looooove sooooo much."

A shiver rolls up his spine.

"Walter Scott?"

"That's him. You were talking about him while you were out." Gina keeps rubbing Nathan's back. Nathan keeps coughing. "We gave you a little something. Makes you loopy and agreeable but still lets us chat it up. You won't remember a single syllable of any of it." She stops rubbing Nathan's back. "But we like it. It's something used for oral surgery."

Hank watches Nathan slip a cloth out from his pocket. Wipes his mouth. Can't be sure, but Hank thought he saw red stains as Nathan clears his throat then pockets the cloth. Hank thinks of the ports. The

TABLE 13   111

ones he saw stuck on Nathan's body in the hotel room the last night.

Was it last night? Hours ago or days ago?

Hank can't be sure of anything anymore. They're drugging him and having conversations with him. What did they ask him? What did he tell them? Knowing, not knowing, seems like a waste of time. He checks his pockets for his phone. Not there. Not surprising. There's no way these two would let him keep his phone.

"Hank."

Looking up, Gina holds his phone near his face. She waves, holding his attention while his facial recognition unlocks his phone.

"Thanks." She spins back around in her seat. Starts digging into his phone.

Hank's blood burns. The phone is the least of his concerns, but it's everything on top of everything. The obvious insanity. The vague answers. The captivity with this layer of kindness with another layer of unspoken understanding. An understanding between Hank, Nathan, and Gina that this kindness could turn sour at any moment. And Hank's actions will choose that moment, more than likely.

His face throbs while his mind churns. Thinks of his mom. Of how he wishes he'd got that envelope of cash in the mail to her. How he wishes he'd never come to New York.

But she wanted this for Hank. Mom wanted Hank to go live his life. Still, in the town he came from, there's not much chance of being abducted by attractive crazy people with seemingly massive amounts of disposable income.

Nathan coughs again.

Gina giggles, tapping away at Hank's phone.

"Finding this fun?" Hank asks.

She doesn't answer. Keeps tapping and swiping.

"Oh, don't worry about your cat," she says.

"What?"

"The cat, at the place you're staying." She giggles at a pic on his phone. "We stopped by. Dumped a bag of food on the floor and left about six... was it six?"

"Think it was seven."

"You're so right. Seven, not six, it was seven bowls of water." She turns the phone showing him a pic of her petting his cousin's cat. "Sweet boy."

"You went to—"

"Your cousin's place. Where you're staying until you get on your feet." Gina waves the phone in the air. "We unlocked your phone with your face before your eyes shut on us. There's a note with your cousin's address and a reminder to feed... Spartacus."

TABLE 13   113

Hank's fingers grip the seat. They've got everything with that phone.

"This lady with the kind face." Gina turns back around, showing him the screen. "This your mother?"

Something in Hank's head clicks.

"Don't." Low and snarled, like an animal.

"Wow." Gina taps Nathan's shoulder. "You hear that? Very scary voice out of Hank."

"He's got some grit." Nathan turns into a parking garage. "We were hoping for some spirit out of him."

"We sure were." Gina smiles and touches Hank's knee. "And boy howdy did we get it."

Nathan slows down, turning to a stop. He pulls a ticket from the machine and the arm lifts, letting them into the garage. Looks to be part of another hotel. Maybe a high-end apartment building. Hank's not even sure if they are still in New York.

"Where are we?"

Silence.

The SUV circles up and up the ramps, passing open parking spaces left and right. Nathan is heading somewhere specific.

"Why won't you tell me?" Hank asks. "Is it a secret?"

Nathan looks to Gina. They smile.

"Well…" Gina says. "Let us just say it'll be a secret you'll want us to keep."

"Understatement of the century," Nathan adds.

Hank's anxiety spikes even higher. Seconds from a full-on panic attack. Can't find any air. Face feels like a furnace.

"Talk to me. Enough of the bullshit." Hank sits up straight in the seat.

Gina holds up a hand, letting him know to stand down.

Hank resets. "Please. Can you please just tell me what you want from me?"

"Due time, Hank." Nathan cuts the wheel, pulling into a parking space.

Hank looks up. He hadn't noticed they'd reached the top of the garage. Open air with a view of the city. But not of New York. At least he doesn't recognize the skyline. Hank's not sure, but maybe it's New Jersey.

The floor is empty except for their SUV and a lone, rusted-out van on the other side. The sky is gray. Light rain mists the windows.

"What are we—"

"Okay," Gina says. "We do owe you a little something, right? A dollop of info?"

"We do indeed," Nathan agrees.

Hank's eyes bounce between them. Outside the window, he sees the doors of the rusted-out van open.

"You see them?" Nathan asks.

Hanks doesn't bother answering.

TABLE 13   115

Gina taps on his phone, swipes, then shows him the screen. Showing him she's ready to record a video.

"You," she says through her grin. "You, sweet Hank, are going to kill them."

FOURTEEN

FEW SENTENCES in life can alter brain chemistry like *you're going to kill them*.

Those words, in that order, roll rough and ragged. So strange that it was said at all, let alone to Hank. Without warning, without context, so little meat on the bone.

Gina and Nathan have killed. Done it in front of his eyes. Makes sense they would think those words, in that order, would be an appropriate conversation. There's an ease with which they perform these unthinkable acts. Strongly suggests they have vaults of experience.

Stranger still, Hank's mind—for the first time since before he watched Chef die—has slowed down.

What if I do kill these men?

What then?

TABLE 13   117

His thoughts have reduced their velocity. Stabilized into an even, steady state. Like lines of troops moving in methodic motion. Expressionless but all marching forward in perfect synchronicity as they were ordered. Commanders Nathan and Gina bark crazed orders with chilly calm, yet no one is questioning them.

Except one.

A lone voice. Soft at first but growing, becoming a booming voice inside Hank's mind that will not be ignored. A call that cuts through. Breaks the steady march. Halts the parade. The single, unmistakable voice of his mom calling for Hank to *think*. Begging him to not become like them.

Don't drink that poison. Words she's said to him before.

Hearing her—the softness, the kindness of her voice—he got lost for a moment. Forgot where he was. Separated himself from the world. Not long, only for a split second, but it was a clear break from the here and now.

He blinks. A quick head shake. Gina and Nathan are staring back at him. Waiting.

They are still in the SUV. His two captors are in the front. Him in the back seat like a child with homicidal parents looking disappointed in him.

He shuts his eyes again. Hears his mother's voice calling out once again.

He returns to being the boy raised in a tiny spec of a town. The little boy who went to church on Sundays, even though he didn't understand it. He gobbled hamburgers, loved comic books, and devoured Stephen King and Dean Koontz novels.

In a flash of synapses, he sees his father's hand. Hank holding it as he died. It was only a couple of years ago. A day that picks away at him just like his mom said it would. His father's face still escapes him, but Hank can feel the weight of his passing.

"Hank?" Gina asks.

"Still with us, buddy?" Nathan adds.

In this strangest of times, he can't feel them anymore. Hank can't feel the anxiety, the terror generated by his captors. There's been so much of it.

Maybe his mind has moved on to the acceptance phase. Or the terror has quickly woven itself into Hank's being. Become a part of him now, so it's as familiar as an arm or a leg. He can't believe for a second there—as brief as it was—he considered murder just to please them.

Self-preservation? Wanting to please? What the hell was that?

Gina and Nathan explain in their normal ping-pong style that there are two men in that van.

TABLE 13   119

Describe them as *junky shit trash* that needs to be removed from the planet. Say they have done horrible things and they will do more horrible things if Hank doesn't stop their hearts from beating. Their words. They go on to say that Hank killing the two junkies would get *the plan* closer to being where it needed to be.

The plan? Hank thought. *Where it needed to be?*

He couldn't believe they were hinting this would somehow bring an end to this insanity. Typical Nathan and Gina. Always vague. Specifics absent. Hank knows killing these men won't make this better. As if Hank committing the most inhuman of crimes would somehow set him free.

Don't drink that poison.

Hank looks up. There's a tapping coming from the front seat. Gina is doing something on her phone. He's relieved that at least she's done studying his. Her phone is in a gold case, while his is in a cheap, clear one. His eyes stare out at the van. Mind on fire.

"No," he says, barely above a whisper.

"Pardon?" Nathan asks.

"No." Through the windshield, Hank watches as two men step out of the van. One tall, wiry, and lean. The other is shorter but just as rail thin. "I'm not doing that. Insane for even saying—"

Nathan makes that noise with his mouth. The odd

clucking noise he made back at the restaurant bathroom. Gina touches his shoulder, taps a little more on the phone's screen, then looks up, staring out the windshield at the men.

"Okay, Hank," she says. "If that's what you want."

A second passes. The taller of the two pulls a phone from his jacket pocket, reading the screen. He taps something.

Gina's phone buzzes. She smiles.

"You sure, Hank?" she asks. "About what you said? Think you said *no*, right?"

"What did you do?"

The two men move to the back of the van, pulling open the doors.

"Didn't really have to do much," she mocks, tapping on her phone's screen.

"They'll do all the work," Nathan says.

"No doubt," Gina adds.

Hank's stomach falls through the floor. The tall one holds a baseball bat, and the shorter of the two gets the feel of an axe handle with black electrical tap around the grip.

"What are—"

"You see, Hank," Nathan says. "Those guys—"

"The ones out there arming themselves," Gina adds.

TABLE 13   121

Nathan turns, looking back at him. "Well, they are under the impression you're working with the police."

Hank's mouth goes bone dry. His heart thumps inside his ears.

"They were given detailed instructions to beat you to death. Medieval style," Gina says, putting her hand on the door handle about to exit the SUV. "And leave your corpse in a park not far from here. Ya know, a bloody pulp of an example."

"Or a message, I guess," Nathan says.

"Snitches get stitches?" Gina asks.

"A bold statement either way," Nathan adds.

"Wait." Hank stammers for words. "What?"

Nathan opens the driver's side door. Gina opens the passenger side.

"Now," Nathan steps outside, looking back at Hank. "I've left a gun in my seat."

"It's loaded. Good to go Glock," Gina says. "Point, shoot, super customer friendly."

Hank thinks of his father. The day he died.

"Do what you need to do, Hank." Nathan shuts the door. Throws a wave to the two men.

"Do what you think is right, Hank." Gina shuts her door. Blows them a kiss.

The men are now only about twenty yards away.

Hank's pulse pounds. Palms itch.

The two men walk in a steady stalk toward the SUV framed perfectly in the front windshield. There's an absence of concern in their eyes. A vacancy. Weapons gripped in their dirty hands, ready for a violent act, but their expressions are as if they are taking out the trash.

Pulling himself forward, Hank scrambles, looking between the front seats. Sitting in the driver's seat is a gun. A 9mm Glock. Black steel-polymer. His father had one just like it. It's clean. Looks new. Not only is there a gun, but there's a pair of purple latex gloves.

"Are you kidding me?"

The two men laugh outside. Calling out to him, mocking him.

His head shoots up. Spine stiff. They've closed the gap between them and the SUV. Closer than ever.

Concerns about right and wrong have melted away. His mind flashes to his friend's older brother showing him how to shoot. They borrowed Hank's father's gun. It was years and years ago. Beer cans lined up on a mound of dirt. Hank missed all of them. His father found out. Hank got the second-worst beating of his life.

Hank grabs the Glock. Hands shaking, he holds it down out of sight.

"Shit."

TABLE 13   123

He sets the gun down then pulls on the gloves the best he can. The trembling isn't helping. Not perfect, but the gloves are on with a little room loose at the fingertips. He fumbles the weapon, then holds the gun low pointed at the floor by his knee.

To the right of the SUV, he watches Gina and Nathan walk away. Heading toward some stairs leading down, not looking back. Nathan's back shakes like he's coughing again. Gina rubs his back as they disappear down the stairs.

A clang of metal.

The shorter one is tapping his axe handle on the hood in a steady, chilling rhythm. He reminds Hank of a kid back home. Kid they called Short Stuff. The taller one motions for Hank to come out and play. Hank lurches forward, hitting the door locks.

They thunk locked. Then, with another thunk, they unlock. Hank tries again. Same result.

Looking up, he sees the taller one has a car fob, his thumb on the unlock button.

Did they give these psychos the keys?

Why would they do that? Why would they send them with bats and axe handles toward a guy with a gun?

The hood clangs louder and louder. Becoming more aggressive by the second. As if they're getting themselves ready. Warming up. Their expressions were blank and vacant before, but now they've found some anger, some power. Faces hard. Stares searing.

Hank looks around, searching for help that's not there. No one is coming. He feels the gun in his hand. Getting a feel for the weight. Finger just off the trigger.

He thinks of his father.

The taller one has moved to the right, while Short Stuff has taken a position on the driver's side. Both standing with a hand on the door handle. Hank can see the taller one is calling the shots. His eyes locked with Short Stuff.

The taller one clears his throat. A goofy smile spreads across his face.

"Ready..."

Hank squeezes his eyes closed tight then opens them fast. *This can't be happening.*

"Set..."

He'll shoot the taller one first. His arms are longer. He'll have the better reach to try and grab him. *Am I really thinking like this?*

"Go time, bitch."

Everything slows, motion caught in a cosmic quicksand, but only for a blink. A fractured moment of stillness before everything explodes into a blur. The right door opens a split second faster than the left. The taller one shoves into the SUV as expected. Hank

TABLE 13   125

points and fires. The taller one's chest bursts open. His body flies out from the SUV as if yanked away by some force of nature. Hank spins around, pointing his gun to the left.

Short Stuff stands stunned. Wild, glazed stare. Stunned but not afraid. Been here before. Hank keeps the gun on him. Barrel steady. Hank's been here before too.

Short Stuff takes a big step back from the SUV. Axe still gripped tight in his hand.

"Hey, man," he says. "I don't want any shit here."

"Get back," Hank yells, pushing himself out of the SUV. "Get the hell back, Short Stuff. And drop that thing."

Short Stuff takes a few more steps back but holds on to the axe handle.

"Those two people you're with," he says. "They're not okay. You know that?"

"Oh, I'm aware." Hank stands beside the SUV. Gun raised. "One more time, drop that thing."

"We're just middle people, man. We're nothing. Message guys so important people don't talk to each other. We just gave your friends the info so they could do their thing last night and—"

"Their *thing*?"

"People like to give orders, ya know? But don't want to do anything direct." He takes a small step forward. "Sure as shit nothing electronic. No digital or whatever the fuck. Face-to-face, but not their faces."

"Get back," Hank yells. Holds his aim at his chest. Remembers someone, maybe in a book he read, saying to go with the bigger target. "And for the last fucking time, drop that thing."

"You don't do this, do you?"

"Man, I am not playing with you."

"No way you're one of them."

"Stop talk—"

"Those people? Those animals? You're not like them, right?" Short Stuff's thoughts drift. Lost. "They kill for money, sure, mad respect for that, but they also take side projects. They kill for fun, ya know?"

Hank blinks. The world tilts. So much to process in what he just said.

"No, I can see it." Short Stuff takes another step forward. "The way you say shit. You're not like them. And…" He looks himself over. "Shit. I'm still alive, so you definitely don't have a clue about anything."

Hanks puts two hands on the gun to stop the shaking.

"Paid us both some big money to find out where our bosses are hanging out. Bet they go to that sweet-ass house by the water next. You wait and see." He glances at his dead friend. "Not worth much dead, I suppose."

TABLE 13   127

He takes another step closer to Hank.

"I'll telling you. Do not—"

"Buddy, if you knew what I knew... you'd kill me and start running like hell."

"Why?" Hank asks through grinding teeth. "Why would you say that?"

Short Stuff smiles, breaking into a laugh. A chill runs down Hank's spine. Out of the corner of his eye there's movement to his right, by the stairs. He turns his head for a fraction of a second to steal a look. A fraction too long.

The axe handle slams into his hands.

The Glock whips hard right. His hands went numb on impact, but somehow held on to the gun. Short Stuff has twisted around after his baseball swing.

Hank feels it split the air as he manages to duck down, the axe handle barely missing the side of his head. The blunt end lands hard to his gut, then immediately whips up to his chin.

Globs of white form. The pain from his broken nose returns with some new hurt added.

He thinks of his father.

He sees his face. It's clear as day. The first time since his death that Hank has been able to picture his father's face. It was the day he died. Eyes open. Head tilted.

Hank drops to a knee. Shakes his head hard, breaking loose from the haze. The white blobs grow but separate enough to see that Short Stuff has the axe handle pulled back, ready for another major league swing. Hank levels the Glock. Releases a primal scream begging him to stop.

He doesn't stop.

Hank opens fire. Pulls the trigger until the body falls to the concrete. Hank sits in silence. Motionless. The breeze rolls around him. Gun blasts echo out across the roof of the parking garage.

He's killed two people. The two men Gina and Nathan wanted him to kill.

Questions slam into the shore of his mind. Everything Short Stuff said. About Nathan and Gina. A house by the water. Everything. So many questions and not a single answer.

The movement Hank saw to his right comes into frame fast. Turning, he sees Gina and Nathan are almost on top of him. They didn't go anywhere. Nathan lands a crushing fist to his jaw. Hank slumps to the concrete.

Nathan takes the gun from him, slips it behind his back, then claps in applause. Gina stands holding Hank's phone, camera lens pointed his way.

"Don't worry, Hank," Gina says. "I got it."

"All of it?" Nathan asks.

TABLE 13   129

"Every last drop."

Hank lies on his back looking up at them. Powerless. Gutted. Mind caving in on itself. He killed two people today.

Sadly, today isn't the first time Hank has killed someone.

PART THREE

FIFTEEN
A FEW YEARS AGO

HANK'S FATHER was not a good man.

Like a lot of sad family stories, his father drank, and when he drank, he liked to hurt. Hurt himself mainly, but that was internal stuff. What he really focused his attention on was hurting everyone around him. If we hurt the ones we love the most, well then Hank's father loved his family the most. Hank tried to square the thinking that meant his father loved him, but even a child's optimism has limits.

He watched his father do this for years. This cycle. This pain.

His mom was his father's favorite target, of course. Hank would later find out there were so many things he didn't know anything about. So many times he punched and kicked her. Hank was too young to understand. Mom kept all that hidden with smiles and stories of clumsiness, walking into doors, and so on. Tropes of an abused spouse.

But once Hank reached whatever his father considered an acceptable age, and when he was bored with knocking Mom around the house, it was Hank's turn. He remembers he was eight years old the first time. First time he could remember at least. He had come home from school and found Mom's face looking like a bloody jigsaw puzzle with a few pieces missing. He tried to comfort her, but he started to cry because he didn't understand what was happening. Didn't make sense that this could happen at home. Then, without a word spoken, his father started in on him. Face burning furnace red. Muscles twisted coils along his forearms. He yelled. He slammed his fist against the wall. He slapped Hank across the room. Felt like God had swatted him like a fly. Powerless.

That was the first time.

The second is a blur. The third he barely remembers at all since it was his first concussion. Hank dove into himself. Retreated deep.

Hank fell into books. He read and read and read, trying to escape inside the words. Afternoons, he'd hide in his closet or under his bed. He'd read late at night under the covers with a flashlight. Disappearing into the pages, becoming one with the

TABLE 13   135

imagery of the story. It was magic. Teleportation was real. He was lifted up, moved from his world, and offered safe passage into another one. A better one.

He'd pull his pillow over his ears at night, so he couldn't hear them argue. But he could always hear the beatings. Could always hear her cry. His vivid imagination could see it all without his eyes catching any of it. He avoided his father like the plague. He would go to other people's houses. Stay late at school and help teachers clean up. He would do anything to not be home. He felt guilty. Weak for not defending his mother. Terrified of what would happen if his father got really mad.

When Hank was thirteen, he stormed out of his room during one of their more brutal fights. Blood burning hot. Mosquito fists clenched. He screamed for him to stop.

He did. He laughed. Then he broke Hank's arm while holding a knife to his throat.

The police came after the neighbors called about the noise. Considering the nearest house was a good ways away, Hank's family must have been putting on quite a show for them to hear. His mom tried to tell the police what had happened, but his father calmly explained she drinks and makes up stories. The police nodded their heads in an understanding fashion and left, telling them to keep it down.

Then his father hit her so hard Hank thought she broke in half.

While his arm healed, he continued to read and read. Horror stories, mainly. A lot of Stephen King, of course. Thrillers too. Some Elmore Leonard crime here and there for fun. His imagination sparked into a blaze. He started to write his own stuff. Short stories. Very short, but they were the beginnings of something that would drive him to this very day.

They weren't very good, Hank knew that, but he didn't care. Just getting words down. Getting it all out of his head and into the physical world was everything. He wrote a story about a boy with an abusive father. A story about how that boy came up with a plan how to end the abuse. He wrote several of them. Each one was more elaborate than the last. More violent as well.

Hank told himself it was just a story.

Told himself a lot of things to get through life.

One day, after his eighteenth birthday, Hank came home from a creative writing class that was held nights at a small community college a few miles away. He was bigger and stronger than when his father broke his arm. His father was older and weaker but still bigger than Hank. Hank ran track in high school. Started lifting weights. Never fully recognized that he was really training for a day in the future.

TABLE 13   137

Didn't know what day, he just knew that day would come.

And today was that day.

That day was nothing special. What was happening was nothing new. It was something that had been running on a seemingly endless loop for as long as he could remember. Hank's father got home from the bar—day drinking on his day off—then started beating his mother for some reason or another. More than likely, something rage-inducing like the dishes having not been washed or a meal being late.

Hank and his mom knew it was more about the empty bottles ruling his soul. Probably even more about the life his father wanted that never came true. The way his father was raised. None of those things are excuses. None of those things could explain away or rationalize why his father did the things he did. Hank didn't care about his reasons.

That day, he walked in, saw his mother, and something clicked inside his head.

He knew where his father kept the gun. His prized 9mm Glock. Watched him clean it and put it away several times. Snuck around corners and paid attention to his fingers working the lock. So, when Hank walked in that day and saw his father hurting his mom for the hundredth time, that click in his head was more like an explosion. He walked into the closet, blood running hot yet still calm and ready. As he picked up the gun, he heard that click in his head again. Soft but unmistakable. That was the first time he remembers hearing it, but it certainly was not the last.

He ran into the kitchen.

Shoved that Glock under his father's chin and pulled the trigger.

It was the loudest thing Hank had ever heard. Dull. Booming. Empty after the ringing in his ears subsided. But as soul-shaking as the gunshot was, guns being fired around there wasn't an uncommon thing. Even if the neighbors heard it, they probably wouldn't pay it no mind. Hank's mom grabbed him, covered his mouth, and told him not to scream. A scream would signal something was wrong.

For some reason, in that pitch-black moment, Hank held his father's hand. Maybe it was guilt, or maybe some broken love Hank needed to express. He didn't know, and he didn't really care.

He did what he did.

Hank and his mom dragged the body out into the woods behind the house. They put him next to a tree, put the gun in his hand and left them there. The angle Hank had caught him under the chin could be considered self-inflicted.

Hank couldn't be sure, but he was almost certain

TABLE 13   139

that he saw his mom put food in his father's pockets. Lunch meat—ham and turkey. He never asked, a child really doesn't want to have that type of conversation with their mom, but still, he has to believe she did that to help taint the hell out of that evidence.

Hank burned the story where his main character did the same thing to his drunk, abusive dad. Hank later burned all the stories.

The police found his father's dead body in the woods, mangled by wildlife and the elements, with a gun in his hand that was registered in his name. Face half removed.

It was ruled a suicide.

It was going well. Or as well as it could. Until the father of someone Hank had gone to school with started asking questions. He was a police officer who grew up and spent his whole life in the same town. Grew up with Hank's father too.

In fact, that homegrown police officer was friends with Hank's father. Later, Hank and his mom found out they were drinking buddies of sorts. This drinking buddy, a homegrown police officer, thought something was strange about the death. The *suicide* didn't sit right. Couldn't prove it, but this officer's gut didn't believe that story. He was convinced Hank and his mom had something to do with it. And worse, he wouldn't shut up about it.

He made Hank and his mom's lives hell.

They were brought into the police station multiple times. Their home was tossed whenever there was an "anonymous" tip. They were pointed at around town. Talked about in whispers everywhere they went. The grocery. The gas station. Church. One time, when Hank stopped at a stop sign, a group of kids called him a murderer. Others called him daddy killer. Others blamed his mom. Called her a murderer. Accused her of sleeping around. Some got mildly creative—*That sick sonvabitch Hank Quinn and his whore of a mom are sleeping together.*

This made running the shop almost impossible. It took a heavy toll on his mom. It took a toll on Hank as well. This was when his mom told him he should think about leaving town. Start fresh. This town had turned on him. Not a stable environment for him to live a life.

She asked him if he could go anywhere and do anything, where would he go? What would he do? It took all of five seconds for Hank to respond.

"New York," he'd said.

She nodded, as if she'd known the answer before she asked the question. Hank had talked nonstop to her about his favorite writers and where they live. How they walk around the big city called New York, living big-time writer lives. Coffee shops. Fancy

TABLE 13   141

restaurants. She knew her son was staying up all night writing and reading, reading and writing.

"What would you do in New York?" she'd asked him.

He smiled. The first time in a long time. Happiness and sadness collided head-on.

"Thought so," she'd said. "Then go do that."

"Mom. I can't leave you here to deal with all—"

"Your life is yours." Her voice had been weak and strained, but there was strength flexing beneath. "He lived his. Did what he wanted with his, made his choices." She turned him around, tears streaming down the strongest face he'll ever know. "I need you to go and do likewise. Just do it better. Live a magical life, Henry."

"But Mom—"

"Go slay dragons."

SIXTEEN

HANK DIDN'T REALIZE how far despair could take a person.

No idea how far down the elevator could go.

The reality of it bends the mind. The idea that his fall began the day he simply went to work. Doesn't make any kind of sense. It never occurred to him things could spin in a downward spiral so fast, landing him where he is now.

Tears fill his eyes but won't fall.

The shaking has subsided, but the memories shred on a continuous thrashing loop. All of it plays back inside his head, but he feels nothing. Not good. Not bad. He is not even indifferent. He just watches it in review. It's all about someone else. Hank feels sorry for whoever that guy is.

Nathan and Gina gave him a little something—a

TABLE 13 143

sedative, Hank assumes, given the warmth in his chest, the calm of his body, and the twisted apathy in his mind. Gave it to him when they helped him to his feet at that parking garage.

Hank's body had gone limp after he shot that man. The junkie. Short Stuff with the axe handle.

Nathan and Gina moved him along toward the stairs as his feet dragged lifeless, leaving the bodies behind them. He doesn't remember much. What they gave him put some fuzz on almost everything, but he recalls going down some stairs, reaching another floor in the garage, then the prick of a needle in his neck.

The world went bright, only for a second, then it all went dark.

Feels like floating now. Drifting above it all. There are blue skies above him. A gentle breeze with a bite of chill. Trees are swaying gently back and forth as if stirring up clouds as the sun pokes through, warming his face.

This is nice, he thinks.

Rolling, streaming hot tears race down, clearing his cheeks before dropping to the grass under his head. His fingers grip the blades, digging in until they find dirt. As if he's trying to find a handle in the world to hold on to.

Hold on, he thinks.

Hold on to what you've got, his mom used to say all the time.

They were at a park on a day like today, Hank and his mom. It was after things went bad, but before the police found his father's body. It was a short but nice time in their lives. They still lived in that small house in the neighborhood. Hank loved that place despite everything. A place where Hank grew up, made friends and experienced some good times, and a lot of very bad ones too. A town that seemed to care for one another. A community of families. Sure, there were differences, as with any group of people, but when it counted, people showed up.

Kindness wins, his mom used to say.

In the weeks after they found his father, people were so kind. So helpful.

Until they weren't.

The kindness gave way to suspicion. Evolved into rumors. *Kindness can turn on you too*, his mom would later say. They became outcasts.

Hank had always viewed everyone's kindness with some cynical distance, even though his mom deeply wanted it to be genuine. He didn't believe any of it. Didn't trust people being nice. It was Hank's cynical nature that made him a good writer.

That's what his agent told him about a month before he dropped Hank as a client. He was probably

TABLE 13   145

right. About the cynicism, not about tossing Hank to the curb. Hank's slant on the world and everyone in it probably did make him a good writer. To a certain degree.

There always was this layer of shittiness to all that *nice* back home, now that he thinks about it. They always had this odd, small-town addiction to drama. Smiles with a punch behind them. They want to help in order to feel better about themselves, while at the same time being part of the exciting thing of the moment.

About a week after his father went missing, people stopped showing up. Stopped offering help. Stopped talking to him and his mom. That was even before they turned on them. Before they called them murderers. Before all that, they already couldn't have cared less about Hank and his mom.

But once the tiny-town rumor machine got rolling, boy, then it was game on. They came around all the damn time. The town was over it, then they moved on to something even more exciting. Being a loud, booming member of the self-righteous dickhead parade was the new pastime.

Mom's business started going south, and no one stepped in to help. Where were they with all their wonderful words, casseroles, and empty smiles? Did any of them stop to ask their side of the story? Reach out to his mom or Hank to try and understand? Hell no. They'd had their trial. Had it in their neighbors' living rooms, at the coffee shop, over chicken fried steaks, even on the front lawn of the church.

He left for New York.

Mom told him to go. Went as far as to say that's what God wanted, but Hank knew he could have stayed. Knew he *should* have stayed. Shouldn't have left her to deal with it all. Left Mom to clean up the mess he created, no matter the reasons why he created it. It's all too much to think about sometimes.

His fingers grip the grass tighter. *Hold on to what you've got.*

He left her once. He can't leave Mom forever.

The warmth of the sun passes overhead. A shadow covers his face. He needs to snap out of this. Needs to become part of the here and now no matter how much he'd rather not. He opens his eyes. He didn't know he had them closed.

Nathan and Gina stand above, staring, looking down at him.

"Feel better?" Nathan asks.

"Got to," Gina says.

"After a good nap."

"Everything is better after a good nap."

"Even a bad nap is all right."

"So damn all right."

TABLE 13   147

Hank can't find anything to say. Words tumble and fall.

"Hank killed a guy." Gina says it like she's making a baby announcement.

"Saw that." Nathan matches her enthusiasm.

Trying to look past them—a pathetic attempt to remove them mentally—Hank adjusts his sightline, moving his head to the left so he can only see the blue sky. The clouds. The air moving them, dancing with them. Clouds at a party with friends and family.

Walking on air.

Hank's mind caves in.

Nathan holds up a box, blocking the clouds from his view. It's a cardboard box holding a laptop. Looks as if it was just pulled off a shelf from an electronics store. He shakes it side to side, like trying to get the attention of a child or a dog. Gina gestures towards it like she's the gorgeous hostess of a game show and it's some sort of a prize.

"Time to get to work," Nathan says.

"Time to write your masterpiece," Gina adds.

"A layered think piece."

"Obviously."

Hank stares at the box. The strangeness of it all doesn't even register anymore. His fingers dig deeper into the dirt and grass. Feels the earth stuff under his nails. Takes a deep breath. The world still smells like it should. Fresh breeze with hints of flowers. Sun overhead.

"But first." Nathan pulls the box away fast, leaning down into Hank's face. "We've got some fun to do."

"One for them," Gina says. "One for us."

"What does that—"

Before Hank can finish the question, Nathan slips a needle into his neck. Hank feels himself slip away from the fresh flower-laced breeze in seconds. A now familiar slip. The same sensation as when they moved him from the parking garage. It's a comforting slide into a warm tub of milk. Doesn't love it, but he doesn't hate it either.

Like a boy hiding his eyes during the scary parts, Hank would rather be out than in.

SEVENTEEN

HANK SHOOTS STRAIGHT UP.

He's in the back seat of a vehicle. Not the same SUV as before.

He's in a car. A sedan. A nice one. German something, maybe. His fingers feel the leather. Far different than the dirt and grass. It's night. They aren't in a parking garage or a burning hotel anymore. Or a field. That's about all Hank knows right now.

He's alone.

His hands are free, but his feet are zip-tied together. He gives them a tug with his fingers knowing damn well they are secure. Those two wouldn't let that important detail go by. He looks to the door. Thinks. His hands are free. Sure, he could open the door and crawl out, using his hands to pull him to freedom.

"Yeah, that'd work great." Laughs to himself.

He thinks of himself hopping his way to salvation —wounded bunny-like—and laughs harder.

He envisions Nathan and Gina finding him about a few hundred feet from the car after twenty minutes of crawling, or hopping, and the guttural laughter that would bring from those two. How amused they'd be while trying to decide how to punish him. They haven't harmed him—relatively speaking—but Hank is pretty sure their patience has limitations. Reaching the outer edges of Nathan's and Gina's patience and understanding can't be great real estate to hang out in.

His mouth smacks, struggling to find moisture. The now customary bottles of water are in the cup holders in front of him. Always the gracious host and hostess. Hank sniffs. Smells a lot like grilled meat, not unlike the restaurant.

There's a plate next to him covered in aluminum foil.

Hank peels away the foil, uncovering a white ceramic plate. It's filled with steak sliced into bite-sized pieces. There's also an overflowing, loaded baked potato and steamed asparagus with a touch of melted butter. A folded note rests beside the plate.

"What the hell?" He picks up the note.

EAT.

TABLE 13   151

His body vibrates. Anxiety waves crashing. Feels like he's coming undone.

"Stop." Attempting to command his body and mind to deal with this.

He sucks in a deep breath through his teeth. Feels something inside of him go limp and loose, then lock in place. He's found sudden calm. Grabbing some chaotic form of peace is more like it. He's ashamed of himself, mad he lost his cool for even a moment. Not sure why anything is a surprise anymore.

Think.

Hank shuts his eyes. Forces his mind to walk down a broken-brain hallway he'd closed off. Pulls open the doors to some memories he shut off long ago.

He sees his father's face. It's there. Clear as day. So effortless now.

Think.

He needs to use it. All of that. Everything from that horrible time. Those thoughts and feelings he worked so damn hard to ignore. That he walled off. All of those must be harvested and consumed.

"Stop."

Sucks in an even deeper breath. His ribs expand. Back feels like wings have formed. Stop pushing it all away. Open the wounds. Jam a fork in and push it all up, so it's fresh with the flesh. Make it hurt again. Make it so it's all of use.

Exhales. Opens his eyes.

If he's going to escape, to survive all this, then he needs to roll past fear. Clear it and move into a state of loose observance. Sure, let there be some initial shock to whatever happens next. Allow yourself to be human, but assess it fast, box it up, and move on. Allow acceptance of the relentless crazy to set in.

If Hank lives through this, then he'll go back to the therapists and let them go to work on him. Fix what's broken. But if he dies, there's not much to fix. Is there?

His hands shake. He shakes them back. Breathes in and out. Air feels like fuel.

"What the hell?" Acceptance unlocked as he takes a bite of the steak.

It's amazing, but it could be better. There's a paste of sorts coating his mouth. Muting the taste ever so slightly. Cracking open a bottle of water, he gulps away the effects of whatever they injected into his bloodstream. As the cold water rolls down his throat, his thoughts unspool.

The faces of the men he killed in that garage flash, fade, then return. They flicker in and out like a light switch in his head, flipping off and on, creating a cheap, haunting strobe effect. Faces frozen screams. Eyes and mouths open wide.

TABLE 13   153

Hank makes hard head shakes left and right. Places his palms flat on the seat. Feels the smooth coolness of the leather. Presses his fingertips into it. Stabilizing himself in the here and now. Goes back to steadying, breathing in and out. Boxing up what he can't use and leaving the rest laid out and ready.

Hank grabs a fistful of steak, shoving it into his mouth like a toddler.

"So good."

Music booms outside.

Hank's body jolts and bounces in the seat. Slight rattle to the car's windows. In the distance, but not too far out, maybe a hundred or so yards away, stands a house. A big one by the water.

Short Stuff said something about this.

Hank chews, ignoring the fear that's coming back strong.

There's a party raging inside. A sprawling estate that stretches out along the ocean like a Labrador napping on the beach. Windows are lit up, glowing yellow with shadows and shapes moving, dancing, swaying to the rhythm of high times in a multimillion-dollar mansion rager. Big-money cars come and go. Looks like there's a valet service.

Hank notices that they were kind enough to leave the window cracked. As if he was a dog. He leans in, wants to hear the tunes but also wants to let in some of the fresh air. Breathes in deep. Takes in all the smells. The cool, salty night air coming off the ocean. Not completely sure where he is, but he's guessing they are in the Hamptons or something like it.

Not out of the question they're farther down the east coast or, hell, even the west coast. Hank's not sure what day it is, let alone how far they've traveled, but one thing is certain, they aren't here randomly. There's a reason.

Always a reason with these two.

That now familiar chill crawls up Hank's spine. Sure, Nathan and Gina came here for a reason, but they are not in the car with Hank. They gave no odd banter before they left.

They're out there. Somewhere.

Plotting, or worse, executing a new plan. The haze of the injection, the diversion created by the glory of the steak on his tongue, and the growing seeds of acceptance of what's happened have all clouded Hank's thinking.

He looks around, scanning the area, looking for them. Nothing. They came to this party and left him here.

Why?

In the distance, to the right, he sees them. At least he thinks it's them. The way they walk is familiar. Unmistakable. Can't make out their faces, but there

TABLE 13   155

are two shadowy figures with arms wrapped around one another moving toward the house. Look like ghosts floating in the dark. There's a gliding strut to the way they move. Confidence mixed with a complete absence of fear or concern. Two people walking through life as if they have the answer key to the test.

They're at the front door of the party now. Hanks holds his breath.

They don't knock, just walk inside.

That cool acceptance of this insanity that Hank had moments ago melts away. His machine gun heart and rolling waves of anxiety have returned in full force.

He's not his father's son. Not a monster from birth.

Hank screams out. A long, wailing warning. One that's been sitting, waiting to be released for far too long. His throat shreds, fading out into a ragged breath. Looking down, he sees his fingernails have dug into the front seat. Face feels like fire.

His fingers fumble, pulling at the door. He spills out into the grass, legs bound at the ankles. Dragging himself, digging into the ground, using all the strength he has from his arms, back, and shoulders, he moves forward inch by inch. Picks up some speed, getting better at the movement. Inches become feet. Looking up through the massive glass windows, he can almost see them moving through the party. Window to window, they move like the apex predators they are.

"No. No. No."

Helpless, but he has to try. He needs to warn everyone in that house.

Run. Hide. Your killers are footsteps away.

A part of Hank becomes unhinged. Primal. He screams out again, pounding his fists into the dirt. The music continues to thump and boom. He can feel the bass vibrate his chest. No one can hear anything he's doing. There's a loud splash in a pool as the beat drops before the music explodes again. People are laughing and yelling as the party cranks up to a new level. He can scream all he wants, but they won't hear him no matter what he does.

Looking down, he sees the earth caked between his fingers, then checks the distance between him and the house. His original assessment was dead-on. Anything he does is useless. There's no way he can get there in time. Even if he did, what the hell would he do? They are going to alter the course of the lives of everyone in that house.

But Short Stuff made it sound like these people are part of something. Something sinister. From the little he said, it seemed like this party has something to do

TABLE 13   157

with the people who fund Nathan and Gina. Who maybe give them orders to kill.

Are they killing their bosses? Clearing debts? Cutting ties?

What did Nathan ask him? *Are you a product of everything beyond your fingertips?*

Pushing himself up from the ground, he watches for Nathan and Gina. Numbness kicks in. Self-preservation overrides panic. He looks back to the sedan. It's a BMW. At least he was right about that. Sure, but he's also right about it being bad if they come back and find him on the ground trying to escape.

The lights in the house go out.

Music stops.

The silence is deafening.

Screams rip. Coming from within the house. Glass breaks. Shouting. The sounds of terror roll out along with the ocean waves. Hank squeezes his eyes shut.

He hears his mom's words to him as they laid his father's body down in the woods.

This is how this was always going to end.

Hank pulls himself back toward the car as fast as he can. Scrambling, grabbing, yanking at the ground, fighting for every foot. Sounds of chaos swirl behind him.

Hank can't help it. He looks back. A man and woman are running out of the house. Nathan and

Gina will be here any second. Hank pulls himself toward the car with all he has. Spit flies, fighting for every foot. He looks back, checking how much time he has. Gauging the distance between him and his captors. They're gaining ground fast.

Two gunshots ring.

The man's and woman's heads whip back. Bodies lurch forward, falling to the ground. Hank stops. Was that them? Doubtful, now that he thinks about it. Nathan and Gina don't run away. Flames light up, dancing just beyond the glass of the windows. Flames start to rage inside the house.

Nope. That's not Nathan and Gina lying dead in the grass. Not that lucky.

Hank pulls himself up, sliding back into the car. Feet hang, dangling off the side. Disgusted with himself for even trying. *What the hell was I thinking?* Guilt overriding reason. He did the best he could, but it was nothing.

Can't believe he's sitting there watching the end of it all. His thoughts become hard and callused. A version of himself that's becoming more unfeeling by the second. A version of Hank he never thought possible. He cried for days after his father died. The weight of guilt hung like an anchor around his neck.

He's becoming more and more comfortable with death. Slaughter. Being surrounded, swallowed up by

TABLE 13   159

killers and the act of killing. Product, meet environment.

The fire spreads. More gunshots blast.

Looking down, he inspects his hands and clothes. Dirt. Grass. They can't find him like this. He stands up outside the car doing his best to brush off his clothes. Frantic swipes, as if he's being attacked by a swarm of wasps. Hops up and down.

He's running out of time.

Judging by the growing quiet, they'll be back soon. Does a quick scan of his shirt and pants, brushes off some clogs of dirt from the back seat, then kicks his shoes against the bottom of the door frame, trying to knock loose any evidence of his travels.

The fire lights up the night sky, spreading out and up like a giant candle stuck into the sand just off the water.

Hank climbs back into the back seat. Shuts the door as quietly as he can, pulling it closed until he hears a click of metal on metal.

Takes a breath. The door flings open.

"Tired?" Gina leans on the door.

Hank freezes. Shock seizes control. Doing his best act, he shakes his head *no*. Tries to explain, looks at her, then stops. It's a waste of time. His mouth hangs open. Words taken from him.

Gina is covered in blood.

Splatters that look black under the moonlight. Flickers of light from the flames illuminate her animal stare. An unforgiving, searing gaze zeroed in on Hank as if he's everything wrong in the world.

"I'm... I'm sorry," slips out from his trembling lips.

"No shit."

Gina jams a needle into his neck. Her thumb pushes down the plunger.

Hank's world resets to a new steady state. That dropping sensation. Falling, slipping, but catching himself in quick jerks of consciousness before everything slides into the dark. In the dissolving moments before the real world fails him, he thinks of what's to come. What the future holds for Hank Quinn.

His future with the angels of death.

A product to do with what they please.

EIGHTEEN

LIGHT.

Blindingly bright and soft at the same time.

Softened into a dull, flesh-colored light through his closed eyelids. His eyes flutter, then shut tight as fast as they opened.

Cracking them open one more time, the pain in his head is immediate. Sharp. Not the same gentle, soft landing he woke to in the SUV. This is beyond harsh. Pushes past the worst hangover he's ever known.

He remembers a party back home. Kegs and red punch mixed in a metal trashcan by a moose of a dude with a wooden oar from a boat. Those parties were always at a deer lease that someone's dad or uncle owned. Trucks and beat-up cars lined up in a field with a bonfire raging, along with everyone's hormones.

A girl kissed him and then held his hand. Emily was in his Chemistry class. Hank had no idea she even knew his name, let alone gave a damn about him.

Hank smiles. The smile hurts, but the memory is a good one.

He and Emily dated until the end of the year, then she went off to college—Texas Tech—and the reality of his homelife came back. *The sickness*, his mom later called it. The sickness his monster father had. Hank had held his father's hand, watching the ending of it all. The sickness that made him a monster being cleansed.

Funny. Hank thinks about all that time he struggled to see his father's face. What a seemingly pointless exercise. Now, *all* he sees is his father's face when he shuts his eyes. That sick man in all his glory. The new struggle is pushing him away from his mind's eyes.

Emily's face used to be plain as day, even though he hasn't seen her in years. Now, her face is as blurred as his father's used to be. Mags's perfect face is also gone. That perfectly framed image hanging in his mind ever since he met her at the restaurant. At the moment, he can't make out anything about her.

TABLE 13   163

His father winks at him.

Gina's face fades in, hovering storm clouds over his muted thoughts. A still, lifeless, smiling face covered in blood.

Hank's stomach pulls into knots. He closes his eyes tighter. Knowing Nathan and Gina are out there, maybe even sitting next to him, is too much weight to bear. It's insane, but Hank thinks for a moment that if he simply doesn't open his eyes ever again, then maybe this will go away. The terror of being with Nathan and Gina will cease to exist if Hank doesn't see them. Just stay here and live within the movies of his mind, no matter how imperfect they may be. Infantile thinking is appreciated right now.

Back at the garage, Short Stuff said something about them. Seemed to know about them. A lot more than Hank knows. The way he talked, it was as if Nathan and Gina worked with—or for—someone Short Stuff knew. Like there was a job they had completed. Again, he recalls with almost perfect play-back how he talked about a house by the water. He was so sure they would go there. That guy has never been more right about anything.

Are they professional killers?

Cold-blooded assassins like in the movies? Old-school mafia triggers for hire?

But he also said something else. Something about

them killing for other reasons. His exact words are fuzzy. They escape Hank's damaged thoughts, but Short Stuff did say something that shook Hank to his core. Said something that suggested they kill because they like it. Pushing down the morality of it, at this point trying to simply understand, Hank's brain stalls, sputters, then starts up in a relentless series of racing questions.

Do they kill for money and fun?

What was the hotel? The party at the house by the water?

What was work? What was killing Chef? play?

Why do they want me?

Grinding his teeth, he recalls every painful detail.

Table thirteen. Chef.

Think, Hank. Think.

The violent ends of the two men from the van. The taller one falling to the concrete of the parking garage. The bullets exploding the flesh of Short Stuff Gina capturing a video of it all.

Think!

Hank resets. Shoves the fear aside. There were medical ports on Nathan's body. He was coughing up blood.

"What does that mean?" he whispers.

"Not sure, Shakespeare," Gina says. Her voice is soft and sweet. Hank feels her playing with his hair,

TABLE 13   165

fingernails lightly scratching his scalp. "Whatcha working through in there?"

Hank forces his eyes open. Sunlight cuts through the room in thick slots. His eyes instantly water. Blinking away the tears, he rubs his sight clear. Gina straightens, standing up above him, framed in the light like the angel of death he knows her to be.

She's recently showered. The sides of her buzzed hair look damp in the light. She's dressed in a faded pink, Pink Floyd T-shirt, dark jeans, and bare feet. Her toenails are bright pink, with foam toe spacers spreading them so they don't touch.

"What do you think?" she asks, wiggling her toes the best she can. "Just did them up nice."

Hank sits up. Too fast. Dizzy, head spinning like a top. Looking around, he sees he's in a bed inside a light-blue colored room he doesn't recognize. Out the window are trees that sway under the sun shining bright.

"Where are we?"

Gina smiles, turns on the balls of her feet, then picks up a tray. There's a tall glass of water along with a grilled chicken breast, brown rice, and what looks like steamed broccoli.

"I love this place. My favorite one, actually." She sets the tray down in front of Hank, then unfolds a napkin, tucking it into the collar of his shirt. "So peaceful out here and fun too."

Hank looks down at the food and then back up at Gina. His face a blank canvas.

"Fun?"

"Oh yeah." Almost purring. "You can do anything out here. No souls within miles."

Looking around her, he sees a high-back leather chair in front of a desk with a laptop, yellow legal pads, and a cup full of pens. He sits up higher to get a better look around the room.

There's a clink of metal.

He moves the tray to the side and pulls back the covers. His ankle has an inch-wide metal cuff locked around it. Loose, but not loose enough. A heavy chain is attached to it. Hank's eyes follow the chain that runs down off the bed, secured at some unknown location under the bed.

Leaning to one side, he sees that the bed has no posts. No headboard. As if it's floating above the floor. He moves the chain back and forth. There must be a center post under the bed holding it up so he can move around the room. *Did they have this made special?*

Gina shrugs.

Nathan enters the room.

"Look who decided to join the living." Nathan

TABLE 13   167

coughs but smiles through it. "How did you sleep? Get some good rest?"

He adjusts his silver Patagonia vest, then works the collar of a black button-down shirt under it. Always looking his best. The cuffs of his perfect jeans cover the tops of his vintage Air Jordans. The dynamic between the two of them couldn't be clearer. The roles. The dreamer mind of Gina coupled with the analytic, *business is business* mind of Nathan. Both playing their part. Both homicidal and beautiful in their own way.

"He's a little groggy, I think," Gina says.

"Think you're right," Nathan agrees.

"What... what is happening?" Hank's mind splits in two. Half of his consciousness is intact, the other floating above him watching everything get more and more unbelievable with each tick of the clock. "What is this? Why am I chained to—"

"Fair questions." Nathan nods.

"Of course. Really reasonable to question all this." Gina nods as well.

Gina covers Hank's leg with the blanket. She places the tray back in front of him, then taps his nose as if he's a silly child. Nathan coughs and wipes the blood from his lips. Gina rubs his back.

"You need to eat, buddy." Nathan's voice is shaky at first. He clears his throat, regaining his normal cool. "You need to keep your strength up, but here's the short version." He motions for Gina's turn.

"A rip the Band-Aid off version so you can grind through it on your own time." Gina claps her hands. "But you do need to eat up. Need to power up. There's labor to produce."

Hank blinks. *Labor?*

"You see, buddy. I'll end the suspense." Nathan's eyes are kind and warm. "I'm dying." He puts up a hand. "Please, you don't need to bother with the obvious social graces."

"We appreciate your concern," Gina says, "we truly do."

"But what we do need is a lasting record."

"Something documenting our time. Something that will live on."

"A legacy," Nathan says.

"Yes." Gina snaps her fingers. "That's the word. A legacy is needed."

"A legacy that you'll craft, Hank."

"With your gorgeous mind and pretty fingers."

"I don't..." Hank shakes his head. "I don't understand. I don't understand any of this." Anger spikes. "What *you* need? Is that a joke? *I* need to go home. You kidnapped me. You took me away from my life. Do you understand that? What the fuck are you even talking about?"

TABLE 13   169

Nathan and Gina let silence fill the room like a balloon.

They stand expressionless, staring back at Hank with eyes boring through him. Disappointed parents letting their boy think for a moment.

Reality hits Hank like a freight train. He's chained to a bed in an unknown location with two psychopaths. That's what's happening. That's his life. Fighting won't help. Making them mad is worse. He needs them more than they need him. They will feed him or not feed him. Let him live and breathe or gut him like a fish just to watch him die.

But they did say they needed me.

Why?

Hank takes a sip of water. "I'm sorry. This is all... This is a lot, ya know? I lost myself for a second there."

"Don't be so hard on yourself, buddy," Nathan says. "This is tough stuff."

"It's a lot," Gina agrees. "Sharp edges to digest."

"Right." Hank sits up in bed. "What do you want from me?"

"To be clear, you're finished with your little tantrum?" Gina asks.

"We can wait if you need a little more time," Nathan adds.

Hank nods, letting them know he's okay now. *Tantrum* complete.

"Okay," Nathan says. "If I may continue, I'm dying, and we need you to record our lives." Nathan motions to the desk and laptop. "We were so happy when you told us you're a writer."

Hank can't believe it. Feels his stomach drop through the floor.

"Not a huge God person, as you might imagine, but learning that you're a writer was such a blessing," Gina says. "A perfect, shiny blessing."

"So perfect in every way," Nathan agrees. "Everything has come together... aside from me dying."

Gina snickers. Nathan giggles.

Hank's vision blurs. He can't believe it. His table-side chatter. Him sharing with them about being a writer, that what's about to get him killed.

"Eat your food." Gina puts her arm around Nathan as they move toward the door.

"Can't wait to hear your whip-smart ideas about the book," Nathan says.

They slip out of the room, shutting the door behind them.

Book?

Hank's entire body shakes as he hears the thunk of the door locking. This can't be happening. He's still asleep. *Right?* The drugs they gave him are messing

TABLE 13   171

with his mind. Altering his brain chemistry. He pinches the skin on his arm. Squeezing it harder and harder.

Wake the hell up!

His fingernails dig into his skin. Deeper with each passing second. The pain is real, but the world is still here.

Not a dream at all. No nightmare explanation to soothe his mind.

As his skin breaks, blood trickles down his arm and onto the clean white sheets. Looking down at the tray, there is a knife and fork. Both plastic and flimsy. A smile breaks. A snicker evolves into a childlike giggle.

"Those batshit crazy assholes… they are good." He can barely speak through his growing hysteria. "Didn't even give me enough to kill myself."

Hank's fear melts away. His manic laughter levels off. He forks a mound of rice and then shoves it in his mouth. He snickers again. Grains fall to the sheets, somehow avoiding the drops of blood, while his laughter gains more strength. Can't control it.

"Classic."

With his mouth wide open, face red, tears dropping, he's never laughed this hard before in his life. He tries to cut the chicken, but the plastic knife slips and bends. Hard to tell if it's the shitty utensils or his hysterics. Hank has never had a breakdown, but this might be what that's like.

His laughter booms. Rolls on even harder. They don't know he's a killer of sorts too. Different league than they play in, thankfully, but he's walked through life differently than they probably think—sweet, small-town boy from Texas in the big city to chase a dream.

Aw shucks. I don't want to hurt nobody.

His mom's voice is long gone. Feels like his father is with him now. Taken a more parental role. It might be better, given the circumstances.

Hank tosses the tray off the bed. The glass of water dumps across the floor. The food from the plate launches in every direction like a shotgun blast.

The door flies open.

Gina storms in, slamming the door behind her. Veins pop along her neck. One pulsing hard across her forehead. Hank's never seen her like this. This is worse than *the plan* meltdown she had in the hotel room.

"Hey." Eyes bulge big as she breathes in and out through her nose. Holding back the worst part of her by a leash. "Like I clearly, clearly stated, I understand how strange all this is for you—noted, understood— but you need to come to grips with where your life is at the moment."

TABLE 13   173

Gina zips around the bed to the mess on the floor. She picks up the plate and then the chicken, pinching the end with her finger and thumb as if picking up a dirty diaper. She then uses her hand to shovel the rice and broccoli from the floor onto the plate like a broom into a dustpan.

"Eat your fucking chicken." She drops the plate into his lap. "Pull your shit together. In twenty-seven minutes, you start writing your best damn book. Sorry, the best book ever written by anyone ever."

Hank laughs. It just comes out. The thought that they don't know what a failure he is as a writer strikes him as hysterical.

Something behind Gina's eyes explodes.

She backhands him, slapping the taste from his mouth. Before Hank can understand what just happened, Gina has both hands wrapped around his throat. Eye to eye with him. Applying pressure tighter and tighter. Standing above him, she leans down into his neck, pressing full-force with his head pinned, pressed against the wall.

"It's going to break my heart to watch your world torn to pieces."

Hank gags. Spit flies. Lips and mouth fighting for air. White globs are back. He grabs and pulls at her arms. Her strength, the leverage she's taken, she's going to choke the life out of him. Here. Now. He can see it in her eyes. She's snapped.

He chokes out the only word he can. A broken, begging request.

"Mom—".

Gina lets go. He can hear her laughing at him as he sucks in as much air as his lungs will allow. Rolls over in the bed choking life back into his body.

Gina blows out of the room, letting her door slam echo behind her.

Hank breathes in and out. Throat burns. He can still feel her fingers around his neck. His face burns hot, but his heart rate seems to be leveling out.

As his sight returns to normal, he sees the laptop sitting on the desk.

Looks at the plate of food. Half of it has fallen on the bed. Not the pretty plate it was minutes ago. He picks up the chicken with his hands.

Terrified. But not afraid for the reasons he'd think. He's terrified about how calm he is. Calm born from an acceptance of hopelessness.

NINETEEN

"DOES that make some sort of sense, Hank?"

Nathan's tone is patient, carrying a dab of condescension. A forced collaboration, knee-deep in the creative process. It grinds on the last few ounces of Hank's sanity. They've been at this for hours.

For days, maybe. Time has lost all meaning.

Gina covered the window in the room. Tacked up a blanket over the glass, then pulled the blackout curtain closed. There's little to no sound from outside. Birds chirping are a treat. Day and night are the same inside this room.

They told him sunlight would be rewarded when sunlight was earned.

Hank had slept slumped over at the desk and was awoken by pancakes served by Gina with a punishing smile. His chain doesn't reach the door.

Not surprising. His only moments of *freedom* are showering and using the restroom.

Freedom that is timed. Monitored closely.

There's a hook on the wall where they place a mirror, then take it away when he's finished on the off-chance Hank finds a way in there when they aren't looking. They are always looking. Gina or Nathan hands him a plastic basket with deodorant, a toothbrush, and toothpaste. They even hand him what they consider an appropriate amount of toilet paper. They tell him when to shower. Sometimes it seems like he's bathing two or three times a day, but he's not sure. They even shut down the date and time on the laptop, which they take with them when they feel they've *reached a stopping point.*

Gina will mess with his hair to make him presentable after he's done bathing. She also shaves him. The shaving has become some of the most uncomfortable moments for Hank—even more than everything else. Nathan is always in the room. Watching as Gina slides and crawls across Hank's body. Snakelike, coiling, sliding across him. Getting close, breathing softly in his ear. Her perfume is flowery and sweet. She gently touches his face. His neck.

Hank tries not to look at Nathan, but he's caught the look on his face. Gina does this as a show to make

TABLE 13   177

him jealous. It's obvious. Hank has heard them through the walls. Sounds of arguing, then the rattle of angry sex after each shave. The walls thump. There are screams mixed with moans that build and build before ending, fading into quiet.

Hank thinks he heard her say his name during sex, then a loud slap from Nathan. He thinks it was Nathan. No way to be sure.

When Gina does this shave-dance, she never says a word, but she keeps her back to Nathan as much as possible. Blocking his view. Then she will lock eyes with Hank and bite her lip every so often. Hank never knows how to respond. What to do. Does he look away? Stare at her? He knows Nathan is locked on them like a missile waiting to fire. Never missing a thing. As uncomfortable as Hank is during these moments, if he's being honest, as insane as this dirty flirting is, it has become an uncomfortable yet thrilling highlight of his time here.

"Hank?" Nathan asks.

Hank snaps out of thinking of Gina giving him a shave. Slipping away from his trance, he looks up at Nathan, who's standing over him, leaning on the deck. Hank's back aches. Legs feel like cement. He hasn't stood up from this chair in who knows how long.

Focus has come and gone. Hank was dialed-in

earlier. Faking laser-focus to appease the gods. Trying to play along and shine it on for his captors. Thinking a positive attitude might buy him some credibility. Purchase some wiggle room that might give him the space to plan an escape. He's looked for weapons. Anything he could use.

So far, no good.

Gina and Nathan have been hovering around him the whole time. Pacing. Talking back and forth. Telling stories, reminiscing about all that they've done, like an old couple reviewing the good old days. They've told the story of how they met. Their first date. The first time they kissed.

Problem is, they've told at least five versions of this love story.

Of every story, really. Each one different from the last. Very different. Neither one acts as if this is strange. One will change the story, and the other will go along with it. Hank has no idea which one is the truth.

The only consistent story they've told is of the first time they made love. This, so far, has been the only time there was a hint of an argument between them, however. The details—and there were so many details—they both agreed on. It was the term they couldn't agree on.

TABLE 13   179

Nathan started by describing the moment as the first time they *made love*.

Gina laughed and said it was the first time they *fucked*.

Nathan thought that cheapened a beautiful moment. Gina disagreed and said their love wasn't defined by something as common as *making love*. That it was bullshit for suburban whatever's. Nathan took offense that she was calling their sex common. Gina explained that was not what she was saying at all. Far from it, she went on to describe their sex together as something that common people could only dream of. *War of pleasure*, she called it. What she meant, she explained, was that calling it *making love* was an outdated, common phrase. She went on to say when they have sex, or fuck, it is a visceral work of art.

Nathan liked that. They agreed on saying that when they *fuck* it is a visceral work of art.

There was no such argument about their first kill. Or their second. They also went on to talk about the first time they got paid for it. The detail. The joy taken in sharing those details, it bothered Hank at first, but now he feels nothing.

Hank has never written so many words in one sitting. His fingers scrambling to keep up with the relentless pace of Nathan and Gina telling their stories.

"Okay," Gina says.

"Where did we leave off?" Nathan stops to cough, then wipes the blood from his lips.

Gina rubs his back. Nathan excuses himself from the room.

"Can I stand?" Hank asks. "Take a little break?"

"Of course." Gina takes a step back. "We're not monsters."

The chain around Hank's leg clinks and clanks as he stands up from his chair, moving away from the desk. Stretching his aching back, he locks his fingers, pushing his arms above his head. All his muscles are stiff and screaming. Can't feel if his feet are attached to his legs.

He hasn't seen daylight or another person in who knows how long. The chain around his ankle feels like it weighs a thousand pounds. Gina steps into him and runs her finger from his jawline to his lips.

"You might need another shave soon." Her eyes are soul-melting.

"Okay."

"Would you like that?"

"That's... it's your call." Hank swallows. "I just work here."

"Funny." Gina steps back. "You're a funny man."

She looks to the door, checking on Nathan's

TABLE 13   181

return. There's a hard, choking cough from the other room.

"Is he okay?"

"Of course not." Gina turns back to Hank. Steps a little closer again. "He's dying. Remember?"

"You don't seem concerned."

"Of course I'm concerned. Again, not a monster. I'm super sad about it. But there's a plan."

"A plan?"

"Always a plan." Gina cocks her head. Smiles. "You didn't really answer my question."

"What question?"

"The shave. Do you like it when I shave your face, Hank?"

Hank looks away. No way to answer this correctly.

"Come on now. I know you do. Nothing could be more obvious." Nods to his crotch. "I used to be a dancer. Did you know that? In a club. Ya know, dancing doll without clothes." Gina snickers. "So, I know what I'm talking about. Any idea how many half-baked, unanswered erections I've glided across—"

"Okay," he blurts, desperate to change the subject. "How about—"

"Did you like when I choked you?" Eyebrows bouncing. "Ya know, that one time."

Hanks looks away again.

"Does this make you nervous?"

"Yes, it does."

"Ask me about the dancing." She straightens up, face fake-serious. "For the book."

"Fine." Clears his throat. "When did you stop... performing?"

"About a year ago. That's how Nathan and I met."

"Really?" Hank registers this as the sixth different version he's heard of how they met.

"He was my best client before he swept me up and away from all that debauchery."

Her eyes slip to the door. She's heard something. She takes two big steps away from Hank. Nathan walks back into the room. His face shifting from purple to crimson. Eyes watering. He adjusts his shirt and vest.

"I was just telling Hank about how we met."

"Oh? Did we not cover that?" Nathan asks.

"We did not," Gina answers.

"Did that shock you, Hank?"

"No." Almost breaks his eyes to keep them from rolling. "It's interesting. Not sure I would have guessed that."

"Sure." Nathan coughs again. He seems weaker than when Hank first met him. More human than

TABLE 13   183

psycho god. "I guess you never would guess we were high school sweethearts."

Hank fights flashing a *what the hell?* look on his face. Forces a nod.

"We grew up in the same shitty trailer park," Nathan says. "Same homeroom freshman year."

"Known each other our whole lives. I'm only a few months older," Gina adds.

Hank stares back. A blank sheet of paper. Room silent.

"That's so nice," Hank finally says. "We should put that in the book."

"Yes." Nathan claps his hands, then coughs hard. Fights through it. "A true American love story."

"Of course." Gina beams. "That's what missing. An emotional core for the readers to attach to." She rubs Nathan's back while he braces himself with a hand on the wall. "This is why Hank is here."

"We made the right choice," Nathan says.

"Absolutely," Gina agrees.

TWENTY

IT HITS HANK LIKE A THUNDERBOLT.

He needs to lean into this. Treat this like a real project. A real book. Gain their confidence, wait, then maybe they will let their guards down at some point and he can get the hell out of here. Nathan and Gina have made the rules. The rules that there are no rules. They make their own truths, and they change them in real-time.

Maybe he can manipulate Gina somehow. Use this weird jealousy fetish to his advantage.

Are you a product? It's their only code. The only philosophy Hank can piece together for these people. They live by the popular, snarky question–are you a product of your environment, or is your environment a product of you?

Think.

TABLE 13   185

Maybe I can turn their game on them. Flip the world on the alphas. The apex predators.

Gina's story of how they met. Nathan's story of how they met. Which of them is true? Are they both true to a certain degree, or is the truth still yet to be told. Gina likes making Nathan jealous. Nathan is obviously sick. But is there a single thing Hank can trust about anything?

Think. There has to be something I can use.

They only take the chain off when he's in the bathroom. Start there. Focus on that. It will take some time, but he might be able to lull them into getting loose with their own rules. Use this shaving thing to his advantage.

He remembers his mom having hard and fast rules about television after his father died. *Killed. You killed him. Stop with your father died bullshit.* His father's voice has become more persistent lately. The voice deep in his skull questioning Hank's own versions of the truth.

Here we go again.

You. Fucking. Killed him.

Regardless, the television rule lasted for a while, but Hank's childlike phycological warfare, combined with his mom's fading focus on the matter, was able to wear her down into letting him watch more and more. He was able to stay up later and later.

A simplistic example, but the theory is the same.

Hank knows he needs to sit back down in his chair like a good little writer boy and begin writing this masterpiece of shit. And do it now. He rips through a sketch of a plan in his mind. Broad strokes. Loose in spots, but a plan of his own is forming. His brain starts and stops, finding scraps of quick ideas. Nothing is out of bounds right now. If he doesn't think fast, he'll never get out of this alive. Ideas flip one after the other like playing cards.

"Hank."

Nathan's voice tears through, cutting into Hank's thoughts.

How much time has passed?

"Let's start again," Nathan says. "Our time needs to be respected."

"Time is a luxury for all of us," Gina adds.

They have a plan. Always talking about *the plan.*

Hank's plan has become clear.

Pick your moments. Don't challenge these crazy assholes. Then, when the time comes, do whatever the hell you have to do to make them a product of you.

"Absolutely. Time is our friend and our enemy." Hank takes a seat at the desk. Smiles big. Cracks his knuckles, then places his fingers on the keyboard. "Let's keep this energy going."

TWENTY-ONE
NOW

HANK'S BODY IS STILL.

His mind is far from it. It twitches and roars.

Time, much like when he was at that house, means nothing. Time is a mushy concept that can't be measured. No idea how long he's been here.

Fading in and out of consciousness, Hank stopped trying to parse out what was real and what's not. Yet, somehow, he feels tethered to the world more than he did before. A contradiction that makes zero sense to Hank, but it's where he is. As crazy as all this seems, he is far better off than he was.

Feels far better than he did in that house. Working on that book. Strapped between those whackos. There's comfort in that, even if none of this is real.

He hears the elderly man from time to time. And

that other, softer voice from time to time as well. The softer voice becomes more prominent. Not sure when she took over, but he is also not sure he cares. What he cares about is he's being cared for. His body still aches. Pain spikes in places on his body that he didn't even know he had, and his mind is still a jumbled mess, but all that has been smoothed out. A coating of acceptance.

He feels the sensation of being moved from time to time, much like before. All done with care. There will be a jerk here and there. Maybe even a little bounce, but it doesn't last long, and there is no harm done.

The panic that consumed him before has subsided. Vanished, actually. Fear has taken some time off as well. In his brief moments of consciousness, he sees flashes of light. Darkness will open up to a gooey version of the world. He'll see a warm bedroom. Decorated much the same way the living room was decorated when he fell to the floor in front of the old, bulldog-faced man. And even though he only saw it for a flash of a second, he recognizes this is a happy home. This is a place that knows of warmth and kindness.

Even with all the warmth and calm kindness, Hank's thoughts drift. They slide back to something

TABLE 13   189

that happened not that long ago. The time at the house.

He keeps thinking of Gina.

There is no fear in these thoughts, far from it. These are thoughts Hank wishes he wasn't having. Embarrassing. Thoughts of Gina while she shaved him. Her eyes. Her body as she moved over his. Her hands on him.

He's had dreams. Ones he doesn't want to admit.

Dreams. A vision of Gina and him. Mouths and tongues. Skin on skin.

Maybe it was the intensity of working on that book. All the detailed descriptions of the sex between Nathan and Gina. Hearing them through the walls after Nathan became jealous of the way Gina looked at Hank. Maybe it's all of it. Hank tries not to think about her. Fights it but loses every time.

The dreams have become constant. Each more enjoyable than the last.

Hank fears that he's lost himself. That everything he was prior to that night at table thirteen is gone forever. His life—if there is one left—will never be the same.

He doesn't hear his mom's voice anymore.

The name Mags is only the residue of a memory. He hasn't been able to see her face inside his mind in quite some time. And as sad as that makes him feel, he sees Gina's all the time. He can recall every part of her with perfect clarity.

Her face. Her smell. Her body.

All her gorgeous insanity.

All of Gina, all of the time.

TWENTY-TWO
THEN

NATHAN AND GINA TALK.

Telling their story.

They lie.

Hank keeps writing. Keeps thinking. Watching. Planning. Trying to find holes in their walls. Flaws in their defenses. Weakness in their system.

There are none.

Nathan and Gina call for a break. Hank lies back in his bed, letting his mind unspool. They've been at it for a long time. Sometimes these breaks are a minute or two, sometimes they are for hours. He wonders what day it is. If he missed Christmas. His mom's birthday. Is it even day or night? At one point, he was using the meal selection as a way of telling time. Simple things like breakfast means morning, and steak or chicken means dinner and evening. Then they threw him a serious curveball and gave him breakfast three times in a row.

He yanks at the chain that's around his ankle. Testing it. Again. He tests it all the time when they aren't around. As if the thing will all of a sudden come loose for some reason, and he can then run away free.

He pulls it again. The clank sounds like a laugh. Mocking his attempts. His hope. He can hear Nathan and Gina in the other room. Sounds like they're talking. Impossible to make out what they're saying.

Hank stopped trying to eavesdrop. One, he can't really make out anything. But two, he's terrified of getting caught. Every once in a while, Nathan will play with his knife while he's telling his stories. Gina will twirl a gun old west style while she recalls tales from days past. A not-so-subtle reminder of what's at stake here.

Hank has made it a point to tell them what they want to hear.

Agreeable. Pleasant. Laughing at their jokes. Acting delighted by their stories rather than allowing his face to twist into a look of horror and disgust. They've talked about their love for one another. Gina has been more flowery than Nathan, not surprising. They also both talked about the kills in great, glorious detail.

TABLE 13   193

Recalling the sights, the smells, what the weather was like that day—all of it. The look in their victim's eyes. Zero doubt they delighted in the power. There's such a distance between them and the people they've slaughtered. Objects for amusement. To be fair, it seems like some of their kills might have been folks who modeled their behavior and actions like someone who was not long for this earth. There were bad people who stole from worse people. Trigger men who tried to use triggers on people who have people like Nathan and Gina loaded up in their contacts.

The others?

The remaining kills that Hank can't file under moral ambiguity. Well, there are plenty of those. Hank checked out mentally one time when Gina squealed while telling the story of the fifteen-year-old prostitute they left in a dumpster.

Another time, Nathan made dark, pitch-black jokes about the couple whose car broke down on the wrong road at the wrong time. Said they seemed nice, right up until he choked the life out of them. Gina had flipped a coin deciding who watched the other one die.

Hank would pretend he was a court stenographer. A guy simply typing away. Doing his job, removing himself from what he was creating a record of. One strange thing—out of many—

Hank did notice. Not at first, but it occurred to him as the hours passed.

Unlike the stories about their past—like how they met or their childhoods and families--they never gave different versions of the stories about murder. Hank would have to pick one of the ten varieties of their great storybook romance as the truth, or at least some fragment of it. But in these horrific stories of murder, not a single detail ever changed.

Never.

Their *kill stories*—their words—were carefully chosen to describe those days and nights. And those always matched up. Hank started asking them to repeat some parts. He'd stop them and ask them to go back and review some detail just to test them. And each time, they both told the stories with the same details. Never a disagreement or anything altered in the telling.

Hank wondered if those were part of their attention to detail when it came to killing. The way they moved in the hotel that first night. How they went into murder mode at the restaurant. Each moving in perfect harmony.

Did they get their stories straight together as part of their process?

Like using those purple gloves or microwaving hard drives. Did they have other stories agreed upon

TABLE 13   195

in case they were questioned by the police or someone else? Hank is sure they did. Then another thought occurs to him.

Do they keep stories from each other?

Seems reasonable. How could these two have a perfect relationship without any secrets between them? Gina has already shown to be a little *off* with her shaving thing. Can Hank somehow use something, some secret story, to pry them apart? Can he somehow use that to find a way out of this?

Maybe.

He hears Nathan and Gina talking louder in the other room. Clearer too. They are close. Near the door. Sounds like a serious conversation. An argument? Maybe, but it seems like something is being worked out.

Can't carve out the subject. There are broken bits of words. Fragments. Hank crawls to the end of the bed, leaning in as far as he can. Straining, but still trying to stay in a safe place. A place he could reasonably explain if they exploded in through the door. Hank thinks about the time Gina almost choked him to death. He strains to use the outer edges of his hearing. He can make out some clear words now.

He hears the word *plan*.

Hears one of them ask *when?*

Soon.

TWENTY-THREE

HANK LIES IN THE DARK.

Gina's neon pink fingernailed hand slipped in and turned off the light without a word spoken.

That's new, Hank thinks.

The words he heard them say hammer away at the meat of his mind. Turns them over and over. Layering dread on top of dread.

Plan. When? Soon.

Memories cut like a razor. Hank on the couch in that swank hotel room. Gina talking about a plan. *The plan.* She flipped from sanity challenged criminal to raging psycho in a snap. Her face blood-red. Veins plump and pulsing. Scolded Hank for doubting them. For what she perceived as doubts he had that they had a plan. Violently offended by the idea they wouldn't have one. Up until hearing them at the door,

TABLE 13   197

Hank assumed the plan was to have him write this damn book.

Seems very naive now that he plays it over in his mind. They are planning something, that much is certain, but the book isn't all of it. How could it be? There is something else coming. Something bigger. Darker. Hank's teeth grind. Mind on fire.

The musty, damp air of the small bedroom presses in around him like a closing fist. He had gotten used to its stale odor—the sourness of old sweat and the faint hint of his own urine—but he could never adjust to the fact he was a prisoner in some unknown location.

Somewhere in the woods. He at least knows that much. He saw the trees out the window before they shut down the world. Before they chained him to the floorboards by his ankle. Nathan and Gina have been somewhat kind, but he knows they are in no way obligated to be gentle. Not forever. They enjoy the pain of others. They'll enjoy his pain once his utility is used up.

Soon. Time is almost up on their plan.

He still feels the pain in his limbs from where they forced him in and out of cars, SUVs, rooms, and hallways. Can still taste the salty, metallic tang of blood in his mouth. The feel of Nathan's quick strike to the face. The grip of Gina's hands around his throat.

Stop. He hears his mom for the first time in what seems like forever. She's calling for him to cut the self-pity and figure this out. Be the person that gets out alive.

Think.

Hank reboots his thoughts. The math is incredibly simple. The only things between him and freedom are the chain, the solid wooden door, and the two talented psychos behind that door. Simple math but far from an easy problem to solve. Even if he were to somehow bust free of this damn chain, there is no way he could make it out that door without being heard by Nathan and Gina.

Frankly, he's surprised they've gone this long without coming into the room and forcing him to write. That plan is coming soon. That's the only explanation. More to the point, the end of their plan is coming soon.

Think.

Hank has no idea how long he's been here, but he's sure it's been days. Maybe weeks. He thinks of his mom more, wondering if she has even noticed he wasn't around.

Of course she has. They talk all the time.

He thinks about when he taught her to text. It was easier to text when he was working. It was painful, but she was getting there. Far better now than in the

TABLE 13   199

early days. Hank snickers in the dark thinking about it. Covers his mouth quick, so they don't hear him. Doesn't want to give them a reason to come in.

Thoughts shift to his job, wondering if he is still employed. The idea of Mags pops in just enough to send him a death blow. The first time he's been able to think about her too. Perhaps creeping death does that to a person.

Does she wonder what happened to him? Does she care?

Will he ever see either of them again? Kindness, affection, laughing—will he ever feel anything ever again? It all balls up and then bursts into shards of doubt and debilitating despair.

The book. They said they needed him to write the book.

Hank's mind narrows to a pinhole. The task they laid on him. Nathan and Gina wanted—said they needed—him to write a book about their lives. A record. An epic opus dedicated to their masses of murder. A book that would glorify them and their special brand of terror. They had given him a laptop, notepads, pens, circled around him, and told him to write some amazing words for them. It was never said, but it sure as shit was implied that if he refused, they would hurt him. Hurt him in a super special kind of way. If he wrote anything that displeased them, they would go even further.

Nathan and Gina spoke in loud tones, boasting about their various crimes, on and on about how they'd never been caught, how much money they had made and socked away. Cars. Real estate properties. Stocks. Passively managed ETFs. And roll after roll of rubber band-bound banks of cash. They love those. Talk about the look. How they love the feel of them.

Hank felt sick with every word they spoke, knowing how they earned those rolls bound by rubber bands. He's hidden it well, he thinks, but he knows now that playing nice is no longer in his best interest. If it ever was. Giving them what they want isn't going to get him out of here.

He takes a deep breath, climbing out from the bed while doing his best to keep the chain from clanking. Doesn't want them coming in, but his back is killing him after lying down for so long. He starts to pace back and forth. Slow and easy. When he writes, this helps him to think.

This is a new genre for him. True crime survival non-fucking fiction.

He works over what he knows and doesn't. What are hard facts and what are the maybes. The chain and the psychos are hardwired. Except for the brief bathroom breaks.

Each time, either Nathan or Gina unchains him and walk him into the bathroom. They do a quick

TABLE 13   201

check of the room, hang the mirror, then allow him to go in. They stand outside the door typically. Impossible to know if they move to the side or stand just outside the door. Regardless, Hank is forced to assume they stay close by.

This time—this bathroom privilege—is obviously the best time to make a move, yet he feels powerless to do anything while he knows they will be on him in the blink of an eye. He has no weapons, and even if he did, he can't fight both of them. But does he really have a choice?

Okay. What does he have?

Surprise. Desperation. And sadly, a history of violence. He lets his mind play with that last one like it was a sore in his mouth that he can't keep from tonguing.

In the darkness, he walks back and forth. Working it through. All the possible solutions and viable angles. But none of them seem plausible. Despair grows off the idea of staying captive here for an indefinite amount of time. It's maddening. Losing hope is a helluva thing. It's all he's had, and he clung to it like a piece of wood in a raging river. Hope is dying fast.

The book. They used the word *need*. Then, it hits him hard.

What if he can't finish the book? What if he physically cannot write anymore?

His mind digs in on that one. What if he was injured?

Okay, that's something. Give me more.

His hands. What if he injured his hands so that he couldn't type? He couldn't finish writing the book Nathan and Gina say they need so much.

That's insane.

Is it?

Wait. The mirror. What if he hit the mirror so hard it shattered? It would crack, but would it break? He could punch fast, quick strikes with his left hand until the mirror's glass comes tumbling down. That would, at the very least, make his left hand swollen, if not broken and bloodied. He might need his right later. If he has to fight.

Wait. Even better.

What if he could shatter the mirror with his left, then grab a shard with his right. A weapon. It might prove to be difficult given his strength is in his right hand, but if he could possibly do it…

Hank stops his pacing. Starts practicing punching with his left hand in the dark.

Nathan or Gina, whichever was watching, would rush into the bathroom off all the noise. Hank could jam the sharp piece of the broken mirror into his or her neck. One down. Either one of them would be

TABLE 13   203

armed. A gun, a knife, or both. Hank could grab that and kill the second one.

Risky, sure, but not impossible. He can't believe all this time he didn't consider the mirror. Letting himself off the hook, he realizes he didn't have to go this far before. *Pressure makes diamonds,* Mom used to say. He also realizes they haven't drugged him like they had before. His mind is actually feeling clearer. The clearest he's felt since they brought him here.

Hank punches the dark hard with his left.

He has a plan.

Now, he has to hope they let him shower soon. Before their plan, whatever it may be, blows up his plan.

He hears footsteps coming down the hall. Hank gives the dark one last hard left-hand strike, then slips back into bed. Tries to control his breathing. Bring down his heartbeat.

The door opens. The light melts away the dark. There are two shadows standing in the doorway. Nathan coughs. Gina rubs his back.

"Okay," Gina says. "Let's get some work done."

"Let's wrap up the book," Nathan adds. "Today."

Today? That's impossible, Hank thinks, but he doesn't say anything.

"Then after that." Gina moves to the window, yanking back the curtains and pulling down the coverings. The sun is blinding. Hank can't believe it's the middle of the day. He would have bet his life it was midnight or later.

"After that," Gina continues, "we'll let you get cleaned up, and we have a super special dinner."

"And a little dessert," Nathan adds.

"And we have a little dessert," Gina singsongs. "This is a special night for us."

The words *let you get cleaned up* shoot a jolt up Hank's spine. This is it. His moment. His chance. Perhaps his last and only one. Last chance attempt to cram the *environmental product of Hank* down their damn throats.

"Sound like a plan?" Gina asks.

"Sounds good," Hank agrees.

TWENTY-FOUR

THE HOURS CRAWL.

Feels like swimming in quicksand.

At least now Hank can somewhat judge time by the sun outside the window. This is the first he's been allowed to have a view since the day he arrived. Privileged enough to see the light of day. Hank remembers reading somewhere about the importance of seeing the sun and its effects on people. Their moods. Mental health. It can actually alter levels of happiness and sadness. Noted spikes in suicide rates in Seattle during certain times of the year, that type of thing.

When Nathan and Gina take a pause, Hank steals a moment to stare out the window, letting the light soak in as much as he can. Sounds silly, but it does make a difference. He feels better, even while they're dictating the story of how they cut a mom and dad open in Belize so their children could find them after being at the pool. That one was at the request of their employer. They wanted to make that clear for some reason. As if being paid to do it made it okay somehow.

The sun is now starting to set. Nathan's coughing has gotten worse. He's had to excuse himself more than once and leave the room. It's wearing on Gina. Hank can see it in her eyes. There's a heaviness to her that wasn't there before. She barely makes eye contact with Hank anymore.

That can't be a great sign. They've referenced their plan today more than once. Hank can only hope that his plan—along with seeing a little sunlight—is enough to counter whatever their plan might bring.

As Gina leaves the room to comfort Nathan, Hank stands up and stretches the best he can. He wants to keep loose. Anything that might tilt the odds somewhat in his favor. After doing some deep knee bends, he throws a few more jabs with his left hand. Wants his strike at the mirror to be perfect. Might only get a couple of good whacks at it before they come storming into the bathroom.

The noise will be loud. Glass shattering. Shards falling. He must strike, break the mirror, find a piece

TABLE 13   207

that will work as a functional weapon, then get into position to kill at least one of them.

That's all-best-case scenario, of course.

The beauty of his plan, if Hank does say so himself, is that it has layers. Like any good story. If he doesn't feel like he can get a useable piece of the mirror, or if they storm in too fast, or any number of the points of failure that might come into play, Hank can go with his left hand being injured and he can't continue with the book. That conversation will hopefully enrage one, if not both of them. This will buy him time.

Not much. A second, maybe two. Then he'll have to act fast. Either using whatever he has available or just going with straight hand-to-hand. The plan is evolving the more he sloshes it around. Tweaks and variables branch off, forming new plans and variations. None of it is perfect or close to foolproof. Odds of success are only slightly north of zero. But it's what Hank has to work with.

Time is running short, and waiting to find out what their plan is isn't a fantastic option.

One of the few things he did learn in his small-town Texas home was how to throw a few punches. He took his share of beatings, sure, but he gave his fair share too. Especially after they called him Daddy Killer and his mom Murder Whore.

The trick is all about will. Who has the most of it? Who has more will than the other during those moments when the fight could go either way? Those two in the other room have been controlling the situation so far. Ruling his world and every second of it. Hank's plan will break that control, if only for a moment. That's when Hank's *will* better do the rest.

Put Mom's face in your mind. Put that night with Mags in there too. Think about the things you love. They can be simple. Coffee at that place on 52nd. Browsing that bookstore in Hell's Kitchen. Reading. Writing. Noodles. Walking through New York and soaking it all in. All the places you want to go. The things you want to do. Live the life your father never wanted you to have.

Hank's knuckles crack as his fists ball.

There's a sound. Feet shuffling outside. It's them. They're coming down the hall. Sitting back down, he places his fingers on the keyboard and stares at the door like a dog waiting for its masters. He sucks in a deep breath. Holds it in his lungs. An attempt to slow down the world. Counts to three, pushing his breath out between gnashed teeth.

Gina comes in. She holds the key to the chain out in front of her.

"Get cleaned up," she says, never making eye contact while unlocking the chain. "We're done with

TABLE 13   209

the book." Pulls her gun, letting it hang down by her side. "Super special dinner planned, remember?"

Hank's heart pounds. Fear and excitement collided inside of him.

Hank smiles. "I do."

Well, this is it.

TWENTY-FIVE

HANK TURNS ON THE WATER.

The sound is soothing even though Hank knows whatever happens next will be far from it. Not sure soothing will ever be a part of his life again. If he still has a life after tonight.

He thinks it through. Don't rush this part. He wants them to think that he's showering. Everything as it always is. Let some time pass. Gina didn't follow him into the bathroom this time. Sometimes she does, sometimes she doesn't. The bathroom situation is unpredictable at best.

Hank lets the water run, letting it warm up. He looks in the mirror. Not at himself, but visualizing his left-hand slamming into it. He runs his fingers along the smooth surface as the mirror begins to fog at the edges. He wanted the water hot so steam floats out

TABLE 13   211

under the door.

He presses his ear to the door, hoping to hear if Gina or Nathan are standing outside in the room. He doesn't hear anything, but he can't be sure. He must assume they are both standing right there, so he needs to operate accordingly.

Not a movement can be wasted. No pause or hesitation in his actions.

He starts a mental timer. It usually takes some time, not a lot but some, before they get anxious and start telling him to hurry up. Hank tried to take a longer shower early on, more about staying away from them than anything else. It wasn't well received. Gina cut him. It will be a scar he'll have forever. Since then, he's learned to speed things up in the bathroom.

His best guess is that he's on schedule. Not too late or early. He looks at the mirror again. Once he hits that glass, everything will go fast. He will act, not react. He will drive his hand into the glass and move. This is it. Every moment means everything.

Deep breath in. Back spreading like wings. Then exhales slowly.

He balls up a tight fist. No, wait, he'd decided a on palm strike. Can't believe he forgot. What else did he forget?

Get your head right, boy, his father says.

He pulls his hand back. Another deep breath in…

There's a pounding at the door.

"Hank," Gina yells. "Time's up. I laid out something nice for you to wear. Get dressed and join us down the hall."

What? Something nice for you to wear? This has never happened before.

"Oh, yeah, don't worry about the chain thing," she says. "Just join us for supper."

Hank's stomach twists. Holds on to the sink, feels lightheaded. His mind fumbles for something stable to cling to.

"You hearing me, man?"

Hank pulls back the edge of the shower curtain and shuts off the water, knowing he needs to keep the act going. If she storms in here and sees him fully dressed, that will make bad flip to worse.

"Yes." Hank hears the shakiness in his voice. Resets. "Yes, I'll get dressed and be right out. Looking forward to it."

He cringes on that *looking forward to it* part. Too much? Is he trying too hard?

"Cool," Gina says. "This is exciting, right?"

Hank closes his eyes. Heart in his throat.

"Yes." He wants to run out screaming into the woods. "Very exciting."

TWENTY-SIX

HANK OPENS THE BATHROOM DOOR.

Just a crack.

Peeks out. Opens it a little more and looks around the corner. The room is empty. No Gina. No Nathan. The door to the bedroom is shut. The smell of what seems like a beautiful meal being prepared fills the air. A meal waiting outside the room. Hard to tell what. Grilled steak, of course, but there are hints of baking in the air.

Join us.

On the bed, laid out like a flat person, is the nicest suit and tie Hank has ever seen. It just looks expensive as hell. A stark white, perfectly pressed shirt with a black coat and pants. The tie is blood red, made of a material that shines under the light. On the floor in front are a pair of classic black and red Jordans with black dress socks tucked inside.

"What the hell are those whackos doing?"

It was a whisper, but he said it out loud.

"You about ready, buddy?" Nathan says outside the door.

"Yeah." Hank starts to get undressed as fast as he can. He was supposed to be showering. He did get his hair wet in the sink to make it look good. "Just getting dressed. Be out in a second."

"Great. Great." There's a pause. Hank can tell he's still at the door. "You like the shoes?"

"I do." Hank can't believe he's having this conversation as he towels his hair, then picks up the white dress shirt. "Always wanted a pair of these."

"I had an extra pair. I saw you admiring mine, so I thought it would be nice." He stops and coughs hard. "Okay. Hope you like them."

Hank hears his cough trail down the hall with him as he moves on. He tries to button his shirt, but his fingers vibrate. His hands tremble.

This is it, boy. Kill or be killed, his father says.

Slay that dragon, his mom says.

Hanks smiles. The first time his parents ever agreed on anything.

TWENTY-SEVEN

A NEW WORLD.

New unstable ground to roam. They have changed the game.

Altered the environment.

As he tries on the black suit jacket—perfect fit, by the way—his mind begins to rip and roar. The plan he had turned over in his head is no longer valid. Blown to bits in a matter of seconds. He knows he shouldn't seem surprised, but he is. He worked through so many variables, but this was not one of them. Better chance of him catching a crowbar to the head than this.

Hank reluctantly tries to tie his blood-red tie. His hands continue to shake. The silk slips between his trembling fingers. Stopping, his face runs hot, simmering. Angry at himself for losing control. Pissed that after all this he's letting fear roll over him.

What am I afraid of? What, afraid they're going to kill me?

That shit has been on the table for a while, man.

His fingertips bounce and shake. He's crumbling. This is the moment, his moment, and he's losing it. Melting down. A new voice calls out inside his head. Not his father or his mom this time.

Stop! Think. Do this thing, Mags screams with all she has.

Hank squeezes his hands into tight fists. Releases them. They still shake. He shakes them back hard. His wrist pops. Hank tells himself to stop. Counts backward from three down to one. Holding his hands out in front of him, he watches the tips of his fingers for any movement.

Steady.

Back to work on the tie. Perfect knot. Even created a stylish little dimple. As he slips on the Jordans, he can't help but think, *man, these feel good.* Standing up, he takes in the vibe of the look. The suit fits like a second set of skin, as if it was cut for him.

Did they have it tailored? No, that's not possible. Is it? Did they get my measurement while I was in and out from the shit they've been injecting in me?

He runs his hand under his jawline, feeling the

TABLE 13   217

ever-so-slight bumps. Souvenirs from the injections. To his right, he catches a glimpse of himself in the bathroom mirror. The steam is beginning to break. The fog on the mirror lifted just enough to get a decent view of himself.

This is not where he thought he would be at this moment. He thought he would have a shattered mirror and a cut-up left hand, and he would've killed at least one of them by now. Or be dead.

Instead, he is dressed in a big-money suit, a sick pair of Jordans, and he is about to walk into a room where he has no idea what's going to happen. A room where almost anything is possible.

They always said they had a plan.

And when he crosses that doorway, he is entering their plan. Not his. Hank closes his eyes. He pushes his mom's face out of his head. Swats her image away like a mental fly. Does the same as he catches a replay of his walk with Mags. Shoves all that down into a cage inside his head.

For so long he's kept them at his fingertips. Needing to see them. Feed off their memory and what was good and decent. Something to fight for. Something to get back to. It's kept him going. But right now, in this moment, he needs something else.

He only wants his father.

Needs to access that part of himself. Dig his teeth

into it and hold on. His mind has protected him up until now. It flipped through all the good things. Nice moments with Mags. Warm thoughts of mom.

But whatever is waiting outside that door is different. Hank wants all the poison his father had in him. All the bad. Untethered access to all that rage. He wants the monster.

He squeezes his eyes closed even tighter.

Then, as if on cue, his father's face appears. There in his mind standing under a spotlight. Not the image of when his father was dead—his face half gone, his head a mess of gore. This version of his father who has taken center stage is very alive. The memories roll at 3x speed. This father has a cold smile that used to cut Hank to the bone. This father is falling down drunk on a Tuesday afternoon. Passed out on the floor on Wednesday morning as Hank goes to school. This father is beating him. This father is beating his mom. Spit flying. Eyes wide and wild.

Hank's eyes open.

He adjusts his coat jacket. Checks his tie. Sets his jaw. Then walks out the door.

Still thinking how amazing these Air Jordans feel.

Walking on air.

PART FOUR

TWENTY-EIGHT

HE'S NEVER MOVED SLOWER in his life.

A *dead man walking* stroll down a hallway that seems to stretch out for miles. Doors closed along the left and right. A dark tunnel, and at the end is another closed door with a sliver of light peeking out from under it. Hank keeps walking down the hall as if he's in a bad vision of death.

Keep moving toward the light.

Slow but steady, as if he's testing the floor for holes he might fall through. Laughs to himself. Can't help it. He's an idiot. At least he was. He was this idiot who thought he knew what fear was. So damn silly to think of everything leading up to this. Think that anything before walking through this dark tunnel should be considered frightening. That was all fun and games compared to this death march.

A cold spike pierces the core of him. Feet move like they have elephants holding them back. Hank realizes this is what pure fear is like. The good stuff. Not the watered-down kind where you can tell yourself everything will be all right.

Nothing will ever be all right.

He reaches the door.

He hears them in there. They are talking. Not an argument. No laughter either. Only a low hum of conversation. Sounds like dishes. A table is being set.

Places his hand on the knob.

Waits.

He knows that once he opens this door, everything will change. Whatever is waiting for him can't be undone. This will either be the end of his time, or this will fork his life into something unimaginable.

He squeezes the knob. Thinks how he can't do it. They will come for him no matter what. Not realistic to think they will never come down the hall to find him. They left him unlocked from the chain, so it's not like they are showing any fear that he'll escape or try anything. He toys with the idea of running back to the room. Shutting the door. Taking the chair and smashing out the window.

He could run and run until he found someone. Get to a phone. Hide. Anything.

TABLE 13   223

He turns on the balls of his feet. Makes it a step or two. Stops.

Think, boy.

There's no way they'd let that happen. These two? Not likely they would unchain him and allow him to escape out a window. It's more than likely reinforced glass. Or they lined up bear traps outside under the window so they'd snap off his feet upon landing. He'll scream shortly after his first breath of free air.

Laughs to himself again. He knows his future is through this door. Places his hand on the knob once again. Submitting to their control of his universe.

He stops again. Thinks. Turning fast, he moves quickly back to the bedroom.

Flying into the bathroom, he carefully and quietly removes the mirror from the wall and places it on the floor. His heart pounds inside his chest as he places the heel of the Jordans on the mirror.

He can't go into that room without a weapon. Something. That's suicide.

There's a spot in the middle of the mirror. The weakest spot. Hank lifts his leg up, pressing his heel down in the center until the mirror cracks. Not a loud shatter, but it did make a sound. His head whips back around to the door. Listening. Pounding heart in his ears. He moves into the hallway.

Still dark. The door at the end is still closed.

Spinning back around into the bedroom, he looks to find a piece of the broken mirror that might work. Needs to be sharp, but also one he can conceal without slicing himself up. His eyes dance, scanning the pieces as fast as he can.

There's one near the center that looks good.

Maybe even perfect. Picks it up carefully, inspecting it. He smiles big.

This will do just fine.

The edges will cut into his hand, but hopefully, the damage he can inflict on them will be greater. He tries not to crystalize the idea, but he knows he's in *die trying* mode. Not a place most people will ever know. Unfortunately, this will be the third time he's visited this mindset. His father. The two men at the parking garage. And the crushing here and now.

He thinks fast. Where to put it? This is a new wrinkle to an already delicate plan. He can't walk in there with a razor-sharp mirror weapon in his hand.

"Hank?" Gina calls out from the other room.

"Almost there," Hank yells back.

He looks down at his new friends. His new Jordans. He pulls back the top of the high top on the right and slides it carefully down between the sock and the shoe. Practices removing it standing and sitting. Not perfect, but the smooth surface coupled

TABLE 13   225

with the fabric of the dress socks and the shoe make for a good, quick pull.

Gonna have to do.

He moves fast down the hall, getting used to a shard of glass in his shoe. *Concentrate. Don't break it.* With each step, it gets a little easier. He has a bit of a limp, but he can say that's from the chain clamped to his right ankle all this time. If it comes up at all.

Once again, he places his hand on the doorknob at the end of the hall.

Puts his father's face in his mind. Shoves all the good down. His pulse rockets. There's that click in his head. The river of red rushes across his mind's eye.

Rain patters on the roof. Thunder in the distance.

Hank turns the knob, exhaling as he pushes the door open.

TWENTY-NINE

DISBELIEF SWIRLS.

He can't believe he's out of his cave. Left his cell alive.

The walk down the hall was the longest walk he's taken in God knows how long. Even standing here, his legs feel a little weak. Thighs tight. His calves pulse. Shifting his weight from foot to foot, he struggles to look confident and cool, knowing he's anything but that.

It's hard to see, but there's a kitchen to the left and what looks to be the dining room up to the right. Hank cannot deny that the house smells amazing. He'd got a whiff of it while in the bedroom, but out here, the smothering smells of freshly prepared food are almost too much to take.

For some odd reason, tears well up in his eyes.

TABLE 13   227

He's not sure what that is about. Obviously, given recent events, this flood of emotion could be all of everything raining down on him at once. Could be slices of individual things over the hours and days that have passed.

It could be the murder. The captivity. The strange acts of kindness and the brutal shift the other way. Hell, it could be these amazing Jordans on his feet. But one thing is certain, there is no denying this is the strangest, most terrifying situation he has ever walked into.

He puts his father in his mind. The tears stop. His back stiffens.

Moving forward quiet as a church mouse, he reaches the dining room. The room is dark save for two thick, towering, elaborate candles set in the center of a long table made of polished wood—oak, maybe. A white linen runner has been meticulously ironed and laid perfectly down the center of the table.

Nathan sits at the head of the table, Gina to his right. They both hold large, fishbowl-sized wine-glasses filled with a deep, rich red selection of wine. There's an uncorked bottle just off the linen. Hank recognized the label from the restaurant. Their favorite.

There's an empty place to the left of Nathan with a large wineglass filled and waiting.

Hank assumes this is for him.

Nathan and Gina stare at Hank as if they are waiting for him to say something. Something obvious. Like parents staring down a child waiting for the words they want to hear. Only Hank doesn't know what they want to hear from him.

The room is so quiet. Only the soft sound of rain falling outside.

They continue staring. Faces void. No smiles. No frowns. Gina sips her wine. Nathan does the same. Unbearable, itching silence. Hank scrambles to say something, knowing that he must, but what? What does a person say right now?

"Thank you." Fights to make it not sound like a question.

"For what?" Gina asks.

"For what exactly?" Nathan asks.

"For these clothes," Hank says. "For feeding me. Caring for me while we work." Looks down and cracks a grin. "For these sick sneakers."

Nathan and Gina smile at one another.

Relief washes over Hank. Feels as if he is given the correct answer to the question. The question of what the hell he was supposed to say when knee-deep in this cold, dead insanity. Did they really only need to hear him say thank you?

Are they that fragile?

TABLE 13   229

Mental note made. Whatever they cooked up for dinner, Hank needs to talk about how great it is. This is where he is—constant praise and thanks to his captors in order to keep breathing.

Part of Hank is just happy he didn't walk out to find a guillotine. Or some kind of sacrificial table for a devil cult they've failed to mention. Or worse, step into the room and find the cold barrel of a gun pressing to the back of his skull. A plastic sheet laid out in front of him moments before his brains get blown out. Like he's seen in so many gangster movies he loves.

Hank feels a kernel of confidence, a molecule of certainty that they are, at the very least, going to feed him. They may cut him wide open after dinner and play with his insides, but they'll save that parlor game for later. They do keep talking about this dessert thing. Right now, for the time being, it seems Hank is going to try and enjoy a meal with these two wackos. Perhaps his last supper of sorts.

In a record-scratch moment, Hank sees that Nathan and Gina have already finished their meal. No plate next to Nathan where Hank would be seated. No utensils where Hank would be joining them. Turning back, he can see the kitchen. Remains of a fine meal served. On the kitchen counter, under semi-devoured meals, two plates made of fine China sit. Bone white. As do utensils that looked to have been shiny polished silver, now with stabbed chunks of meat and remains of crusted something.

Hank thinks about asking, *Excuse me, I was led to believe I was having something to eat?*

As his eyes adjust to the candlelit room, Hank looks closer at Gina. Her face. She holds a look that he's never seen. There's sadness. She's been crying.

He turns to Nathan. His eyes are puffy. Face hangs limp and lifeless.

The table, this room, has the vibe of a dinner between lovers gone horribly wrong. If Hank didn't know better, he would think this was some kind of breakup. A *we need to talk* style of dinner.

But that can't be what's going on.

Can it?

As crazy as everything has been—the moments of terror, spikes of violence, jumbled, random oddities of Gina and Nathan, then the healthy swirls of mix-and-match stories told for this wackadoo memoir—the idea that Nathan and Gina went through all this just so they could sit down, make a lovely dinner, then break up?

This can't be the plan they've talked about. No.

That's insane, even by their high standards of crazy.

Hank continues to stand. Silent. Back stiff. He can

TABLE 13 231

feel the shard of mirror glass between his sock and shoe. Surprisingly, it is not cutting into him. More like it is calling to him. Screaming to be set free. Begging to come out and play. To put an end to all this.

Even in Hank's wildest of dreams, there's no way he can pull out the mirror shard and kill both these people in some flawless ballet of violence and skill. Doubts he could even wound them enough to escape. Even as he was breaking the mirror, he knew this was more about defense or seizing an opportunity if he was lucky enough to have one present itself.

This was about waiting for the right moment, about having something to take action with if there was an action to take.

"Hank." Nathan's eyes are full. Aching to roll big fat tears down his face. "Join us."

Nathan pulls out the chair next to him.

The sound of the chair rubbing against the tile makes Hank jump. It was involuntary. He'd been so cool up to that moment, and his body betrayed him by showing just how terrified he truly is. The last thing on earth he wants to do is take a seat at that table. But he has no choice.

"Thank you." Sitting down next to Nathan, he tries to visualize how he'll take the mirror shard from his shoe and jam it into his neck. "This is nice."

Hank's father's face pops into his mind. Angry. Disappointed.

Nathan looks to Gina. Gina looks to Nathan.

They reach across the table and hold hands. Fingers locked. Nathan pulls out a tiny box from his tweed sport coat with his free hand. Looks like a jewelry box. Ornate. Made in a shiny black material with pops of red and white across the top like splattered paint.

Gina's eyes flare. Recognition ignites behind them. Nathan places the box in the middle of the table between the two candles. They still hold hands.

Their eyes lock. Tears fall. Hank's pulse thumps like a bass drum.

Nathan's voice cracks as he tries to speak. He coughs, raises a finger requesting a moment, then blood spits from his lips. He wipes them clean. Clears his throat and begins to speak again.

"This is the plan," he says. "This was always the plan."

"The plan ever since that horrible afternoon," Gina adds.

The air in the room feels thick. Like you could carve it with a knife. As if some cosmic force changed the oxygen within this room, the molecules altered in some way.

His mind jumps and bounces, but he says nothing.

TABLE 13   233

He sits, staring at them, taking in the looks on their faces. Sorrow mixed with reflection. This is new. Nothing he's seen or would expect from Nathan and Gina. In this perfect moment, they almost seem human, and it scares Hank even more.

Nathan's and Gina's fingers pull away from one another.

Nathan opens the box.

Inside are two pills. White capsules that look like any other pill, but Hank knows there's no way these are like any other pills. There's an intensity to the way Nathan and Gina are looking at one another now. Studying one another through tears now streaming. Soaking in each other's faces, taking in every detail as if not to forget. Broken smiles, palms flat on the table with their backs straight. Hank can see a vibration in them. They're shaking. They are truly afraid of what's next. They are trying to hang on and be strong for one another during this moment.

Oh my God.

This is the plan.

THIRTY

HANK LOOKS AGAIN—THERE are two pills.

Not three.

Where do I fall in their plan?

The mirror shard in his shoe demands action. If their plan is to take those pills, die, then why not pull one of their many weapons and kill Hank?

Nathan and Gina sit bound to one another in a silent trance. Hank thinks of slipping away. Take it slow, step by step, and move steady toward the door. But he doesn't want to distract whatever this is. If they are going to do a *lovers die together rather than live apart* tragic ending, then Hank only needs to find the eye in the storm, squat his ass there safe and sound, hold on, and ride this insanity out.

"You make sure that book gets out there." Nathan's voice breaks. "Will you do that?"

TABLE 13   235

Hank nods.

"It's everything," Gina says.

"Our story," Nathan adds. "Put this as the ending."

"Perfect end." Gina wipes the corner of her eye.

Hank swallows hard as Gina takes a pill from the case. Nathan does the same.

They hold them out, pinched between their fingers and thumbs. As if they've worked this ceremony out. All the moves are choreographed. They each raise their wine, clink glasses one last time, take a sip in unison, letting the red wine roll around their mouths and tongues before swallowing. Savoring the final tastes of their lives.

Hank can't believe he is sitting here. Watching. Shouldn't he stop them? Say something? Do something? What kind of person watches two people kill themselves.

Fuck 'em, his father says.

Agreed, Mags and Mom say.

Lighting flashes through the windows. Thunder cracks. The rain is coming down hard now.

"Seems silly to say, but it's true." Nathan coughs. "I love you, Gina."

"Nothing silly about it," Gina says. "I love you, Nathan."

Each places the pill in their mouth. Each takes a swig of wine, tilts their head back, swallowing hard.

Nathan shows his empty hand to Gina.

Gina shows the pill still pinched between her fingers. Nathan's eyes pop wide. Disbelief washing over him in a crushing wave.

"Take your medicine," Nathan says. "What are you doing?"

"Couples grow apart sometimes," Gina says. "We want different things."

"This was the plan, Gina."

"This was your plan, Nathan."

Gina glances at the clock on the wall and then turns to Hank. Hank realizes he might have a need for that mirror shard after all.

"I do love you." Gina touches Nathan's hand. "I just don't want to die with you. Does that sound silly to say?"

Nathan slams his fists down on the table. Wine flies, spraying the table. The candlelight sways, altering the shadows of the room. Hank slowly pushes his chair back, knows he needs to make a move, visualizes pulling the makeshift weapon from his shoe. Gina shakes her head at Nathan's response. She looks at the clock.

"You've got roughly four minutes left on the planet, Nathan." Gina tosses her pill at his face, bouncing it off his nose, then drains her wineglass. "This really how you want to use it? By being a dick?"

TABLE 13   237

Nathan coughs hard. Blood spits across the white tablecloth, darker reds mixing with the wine. Gina scrunches her nose.

"Gross," she says. "The second you found out you were dying, you went full-on narcissist. Sort of assumed that I'd be dying to die with you."

"We—" Coughs even harder. Blood drips from his lips. "We built something together. You said *live together, die together*. We talked it through. That first night at the restaurant." Face red, he stabs a finger at Hank. "His fucking restaurant."

"Yup. Table thirteen. Said a lot of things there, and I meant about thirty-five percent of it." Gina leans back, checks the clock again. "Three minutes."

Hank pulls his pants leg up ever so slightly. Doing what he can to get a clean grab. He'll only get one shot at this, maybe two if he's lucky, before the sides of the broken mirror cut up his hand until he can't hold it any longer. Maybe he can hurt her, buy some time and find another weapon in that kitchen.

He makes a quick scan behind him. Looks over the kitchen. As the candlelight settles, through the tilting shadows he sees three large iron pans. A big butcher knife on a cutting board. He can't believe that's all sitting there. So close and so far. He checks the door. He's got a clear shot at it.

His heart skips a row of beats in the best way

possible. There's a set of keys on a table by the door. A fob with some keys on a pink rabbit's foot keychain.

Nathan stands. Wobbles and sways as the poison takes hold.

Gina sits watching. Colder than cold. She plays with the flame burning on the candle. Waves her hands across it, making the shadows move across their faces.

Feels like a bomb is about to go off. Hank's eyes bounce between the butcher knife and the car keys. Love to have both, but not the time to get greedy.

The knife, his father screams.

The keys, his mom says with calm confidence.

Nathan's mouth makes that sound. That cluck or click that he made that night at the restaurant. Gina doesn't return the gesture. She blows Nathan a kiss with a mocking wave goodbye.

Time stops. Everything inside of Nathan appears to break.

He dives with the force of a charging bull. Slides across the table in a blink of an eye, wrapping his hands around Gina's throat as he crashes into her. Her chair flies back on impact. They land hard on the floor, the tablecloth wrapped around them both. Wineglasses fly and shatter. Candles tumble to the tile floor. The room is even darker than before. Hank

TABLE 13   239

pushes away from the table stumbling backwards but finds his footing.

A streak of lightning. Thunder claps.

Gina releases a primal scream as she breaks free, slamming his head against the floor. Guttural, inhuman sounds. Words choked and barked between them, trading violence back and forth. Nathan flips them both around. Dull thumps of fists pounding flesh. Primal. Brutal.

Hank slips the shard out from his shoe. The shard feels wet, and he can see black blood in what little light's left. Didn't even feel it cutting into him. He looks towards the door, then the kitchen, then back to Nathan and Gina.

Nathan will be dead soon.

This is Hank's only chance. Now or never. He tosses the mirror shard aside, bolting to the kitchen. In a single swipe, he grabs the knife, spins around, then explodes out from the kitchen charging hard toward the door. Feels like he's moving in slow motion. Days of lying in that bed and sitting in that chair aren't helping.

He snatches up the key chain and flings the door open in one move. A cold wind hits him. The storm is raging out here, rain pouring down in buckets. This is the first breath of fresh air he's had in forever. There's a car. An Audi A8. The key chain fumbles in his shaking hand. The pink rabbit's foot slides from his fingers.

"Shit!"

Grabbing it as fast as he can, he presses unlock on the fob. The A8's lights flash.

Something hard slams into the back of his head. Puts him down on the porch. His sight flashes to white, then back, then to white again. The world tilts. Through his blurry vision, he sees a wine bottle rolling into view.

Looking up, his worst nightmare stands in the doorway.

Gina is covered in blood. Her hands shake, cut and ragged. She sucks in deep, hard breaths. Wide, frenzied eyes. Something has come undone behind them. Her wig has been pulled off. She rubs her buzz-cut head. Licks some blood from her hand. He can make out Nathan's body on the floor inside the house. He isn't moving.

Hank pushes up from the porch. Gina slams her shoulder into him, putting him down immediately. She flips him around like a child, pinning his arms down with her knees. Straddling him, she grabs both sides of his head, slamming his skull up and down on the wood of the porch.

Hank feels his brain slosh as she releases letting his head fall. Can't feel his legs. Gina's knees alter left

TABLE 13   241

and right, coming off his arms slightly as she punches. There's some feeling left in one of his hands. The one hand that still holds on to something.

Hank slashes the butcher knife in any direction he can. Blind, frantic swipes and stabs. His arm stops with a thunk of blade stuck into flesh. A warm spray flies across his face. Gina roars, rolling to the left. Hank flips his body, slipping his arms out from her knees. Shoving his body clear, he spider crawls off the porch, trips, and stumbles before finding his footing, racing to the A8 the best he can. His feet slip and slosh through the pounding rain.

"Stop!" Gina screams out, her voice cutting through the storm.

Hank stops. Turns around. She holds her gun steady as she yanks the knife free from her thigh.

"Come. Back. Here." Pushing the words through her gnashed teeth. "Now."

Feels like falling. Nothing like walking on air.

From behind her, Hank sees movement. Nathan is moving. He sits up from the floor. Hank forces his face to go blank. Don't give her anything. At this distance, in the driving rain, through her rage, maybe she won't notice what Hank sees.

She curls a finger, instructing him to come to her like a child's angry mother who's not asking. Hank steps toward her, needs to buy some time. Nathan is trying to get up, but his hand slips on the blood and he falls back to the floor.

Hank wipes the rain from his eyes. "What happens next?"

"You get the hell in the house."

Nathan is up on his feet. Foam drips from his mouth, not long for this earth.

"And then what?" Hank shouts to be heard over the storm. "Chain me up? Do that whacko, sexy shave thing, you fucking pervert."

"You love it." She readjusts her aim to his head. "Say it."

"Rather not."

"You're going to beg me—"

Nathan lands on her back. The gun goes off harmlessly into the wood column of the porch. The blast rolls off swallowed up by the storm. Hank launches for the A8. Feet slide, then find traction. No looking back. He can hear them attacking one another like animals.

Pulling the door open, Hank slides into the leather. Soaked to the bone. Mind barely inside his skull. He stabs at the ignition. The engine purrs to life. Puts down the gas. The tires spin before finding traction.

The car lurches forward. Tires spin, spit mud, then catch the gravel. The world is a blur. His mind stuck

TABLE 13   243

in a constant fog. Hank cuts the wheel hard, inches from missing a tree. He can barely feel the steering wheel in his hands. Feels his own blood flowing away from his body and down his skin.

The white blobs are back, taking over more ground with each passing second. There's no stopping now. He clicks on his seat belt. Lighting cracks. Thunder rattles the car. Hank pushes down the gas harder.

A gunshot rings out in the distance.

The back window blows out. Something rips and burns through his arm.

THIRTY-ONE
THEN BECOMES NOW

THE SEAT BELT WAS SOLID.

Did what it was supposed to do.

Stopped him from sailing through the windshield and becoming one with a tree. Kept his battered body from being thrown clear from the Audi.

Friends call him Hank. The people he's running from call him Hank, too.

They are not friends.

They wanted something. Wanted too much.

Even through the driving rain, Hank can smell the automotive cocktail. An overpowering smell of gas mixed with a slight, sanitized stink of wiper fluid. An unforgiving tree stares back at Hank through spider-webbed cracks in the windshield. Rain streams down the bark.

Hank falls out of the car door. Sloshes, slips, fights

TABLE 13   245

his way through the mud and dense woods. Streaks of lighting rip through sheets of rain. Thunder rolls through the dark.

There's a dot. A light. Up in the distance. It's a house.

A kind, bulldog-faced old man takes him in as he loses consciousness.

Hank's body is carefully bandaged. Gently moved to places of comfort. Hank needs time. Time to heal. Despite not being able to fully engage with the *now* and rationalize what happened *then*, he feels a sense of safety here. A calm from being cared for. From being set free from the nightmare.

Time is a memory. Something that once meant so much means so little now. This dreamlike dance with trailing, abstract visions—between what's real and what's imagined—has Hank blissfully unaware of the world and his place in it. A pleasant mental vacation of sorts, considering what he's been through.

He has noticed recently, whatever *recently* means, that he has been more in the world than out of it. There have been true moments of clarity. Still fuzzy and soft. Still sideways, more out than in, but there have been times when he's sure he's been part of things rather than floating around them.

He feels a woman's fingers running through his hair. A soft voice speaking.

Then there's a sound. Something strange yet familiar.

Hank's mind screams out. Panic ignites. He forces his eyes to open. The light is so bright he imagines it searing his eyeballs. He blinks away the globs. Rubs away the tears.

He hears that sound again. An odd noise was made with someone's mouth. A cluck.

"Hank?" Gina says. "You joining the living?"

His body jolts. Pulling back quick, scrambling away from her voice, his back hits something solid. A wall. His fingers feel the texture of the paint. He forces his eyes open again.

He can see her. Gina bathed in light. The angel of death once again above him.

As the blur fades, his focus dials in. She's no longer covered in blood with wide, crazed eyes. She's clean. Seems cool and collected. A few healing scratches here and there. Wearing her pink, Pink Floyd shirt and jeans. Holding two cups of steaming coffee, she cocks her head birdlike, staring at Hank as if nothing is wrong.

Looking around, Hank realizes he's in a bed. Just like he thought he was. At least that's real. The windows are open, letting in the sun and a cool breeze. The storm has long since gone, but there is a hint of something in the air. A freshness after the rain.

TABLE 13   247

"Good to see you all bright-eyed." She sets down one of the coffee cups on a small table next to the bed. "At first, you were a little sketchy. But we got you fixed up all good and proper."

Hank thinks of the kind, bulldog-faced old man.

"What..." His voice fails him. Throat bone-dry.

"Here. Here." Gina hands him a tall glass of water with a long straw.

As he sucks down the water, Gina smiles, eyes full of warmth. She runs her fingers through his hair again. Hank tries to jerk away but doesn't want to give up the water. When he's finished, she takes the glass and sets it down next to the coffee cup.

"Now," she says. "You have questions."

Hank pushes himself off the wall lunging forward only to fall down to the floor. Gina takes a small step back, unfazed by his weak attempt at an attack.

"Yeah. That's not gonna work, darling." She helps him back up into the bed. Adjusts his pillow. "You're still a mess. Better. Soooo much better, but far from battle-boy ready."

The pain returns. His entire body throbs. As his heartbeat cranks, all the wounds start to scream back to life.

"What did you do with him?" Hank asks.

"Who?"

"The man. The man who lives here."

"The old bulldog guy?" Scrunches her nose. "I think you know."

Hank can see it. It's all over her face. The joy of killing. He lunges at her again. Doesn't even clear the bed this time but catches himself before he falls. A tiny win.

"Oh stop that shit, Hank. Can you stop? I've got some things to say to you, and ya know what?" Gina holds her arms out wide. "You're gonna want to hear it. So. Listening ears, bro."

She pulls up a chair, spins it around, then sits with her chin resting on the back. Hank sits on the edge of the bed. Rubs his face. Digs his toes into the rug, trying to get feeling back. His head is clearing, but life is still caught in a thick fog.

"I'm going kill you," he says through his grinding teeth.

"Yeah, well, you'd try." Gina pulls her Glock from behind her back, letting it dangle by her leg. "But you're the kinda fella who brings a broken mirror to a gunfight." She bounces her eyebrows. "But, considering what you did to that mean old dad of yours…"

As her words trail off, Hank's stomach drops. *How does she know?*

"Yeah, we talked about what Hank did to mean old dad. You're such a bad boy." Clocking his stunned expression, she says, "Remember? I told

TABLE 13   249

you. That medicine we gave you makes you loopy and sleepy as all hell. You drop in and out, but you still retain some form of consciousness. We can still chat here and there. Still get some physical aspects out of you when, ya know, nudged along."

"Nathan is dead. You can go anywhere, do anything. What do you want?"

"Hank. I've just lost someone close to me." She stands, shoving the chair against the wall. Hand on her chest as if clutching pearls. "And all you can do is think of yourself? You're better than that."

"Fuck you."

"Funny you should say that." Gina raises her T-shirt and softly rubs her stomach. A smile spreads.

"What?"

Hank presses his feet into the floor. Trying to ground himself. Hands grip the bed. Still has some strength in his hands.

"Nathan wanted immortality. He thought a book about his life would give him that. A documented history and blah, blah, blah." Gina looks down as her hand gently rubs her belly in a wide circle, gun swaying by her side. "But there's only one real way to do that. That's through a child."

Hank's mind splits in half. She steps a little closer. Watching him as if she wants to soak up his reaction.

Devour it all, lick the plate and take in every last crumb.

Hank finds pieces in the deepest parts of his mind. Digs in. Searches. Finds the ones that fit. The fantasies of Gina. The vivid details of sexual visions. Skin on skin. Mouths, tongues, and hands.

"Just wanted a little something out of you."

"You—"

"I did."

The times she shaved him at that house. The uncomfortable, awkward, arousing moments that he loved and hated at the same time. The moving across his body. The breathing in his ear. The soft touches. The tease of a grind. She was planting all of it in his mind. Something to harvest later. While also testing to see if she could excite him.

"Now, the romance was a little one-sided—the fucking, to be clear—but I understand you were a little challenged." Gina's lip curls. "But when I needed you to, you rose to the occasion like a champ."

His mind caves in on itself. Feels his body surge.

"Hope it has your eyes. You've got gorgeous peepers, Hank."

Hank pushes off from the floor with all he's got. His body falls into hers. They tumble backward, landing hard on the floor. He manages to get a punch to her face, then another, before she slams her palm

TABLE 13   251

up under his chin. She twists him free by forcing his neck just shy of snapping. Hank rolls off and spins around, lunging at her one again. He's met with a punishing foot to his chest.

Hank stumbles back, air robbed from his lungs, but he gets to his feet. Gina stands just out of his reach, but she's ready to go. Her feet are planted. Shoulders squared. Broken grin. Her Glock skidded to a stop against the door, out of reach from them but not so far away they couldn't make a dive for it.

"Think, Hank." She rubs blood from her nose. "I'm the mother of your child."

"After all this. After... You think I'm going to just let you walk away?"

"Fine. Cool. But think about it." Runs her tongue over her teeth. "Really think about it. I'm not your mean *drunk* old dad. Think about what I am. You want to go toe to toe with me? On a good day, I'd only kill you. And, buddy, you are not having a good day."

"I'll take my chances." Hank leans forward, a second from diving for the gun.

"Your chances are dogshit, Hank," she yells. "And you know it. I could have killed you so many damn times. But I didn't. We've got a bond now. A strong one." She cracks her neck. "Now. You want to take a shot at the title, okay. We can duke it out. And after a pregnant woman snaps your bitch-ass in two, I'll finish off the leftover chili from last night, burry you out back next to that old man, and go live my life like the queen that I am."

"Last time. What do you want?"

"Just want you to be happy, bro."

"Stop—"

"Serious stuff here. I want you to go finish what you started with that Mags chick. Want you to see your mom." She pauses. Drinks in the look on his face. "Yeah, Hank. You babbled about both of them more than any one person should ever have to listen to." Makes a gagging face. "On and on. Oh my God it was fucking nauseating."

Kill her, his father says.

Listen to her, Mags and his mom say.

"What do I want? It's simple. We part ways," she says. "I go my way, and you go yours."

"Bullshit."

"Can understand you being a little hesitant to trust after—"

"The only way this will end is by one of us dying. You know it."

"Look at you. Trying to control the game. Alter my world. Love it. You've learned things, man."

Gina pulls a knife from under the leg of her jeans. She shows off the blade. It's Nathan's. Flips in the air,

TABLE 13   253

catching it underhanded. A little show to let Hank know who's really running things.

"Here's the deal. I don't want to kill the father of my child. Not above it, but I'd rather not. Seems unnatural before it's born."

Hank stares at the blade. Eyes the gun on the floor. It's suicide.

He dives for it anyway.

Gina moves a fraction of a second later than Hank. He skids and slides, slamming into the wall, but he feels the grip of the gun in his hand. He flips over on his back. Opens fire until the gun clicks empty. The blasts are deafening.

There's a stab in his neck.

Tiny. Too small to be a blade. White globs form slow, then rush in fast.

Feels like he's peeling away from the world.

THIRTY-TWO

HANK'S EYES POP OPEN.

Spartacus is standing on his chest, licking his face.

Hanks sits up quick. Too quick. His head is scrambled. Mouth dry. He's laid out on the couch in cousin Ronnie's apartment. It's dark except for a single lamp on a table next to the couch. It's the middle of the night. The microwave clock in the kitchen across the apartment says it's 2:13 a.m. in a green digital glow.

He feels foggy but surprisingly okay, like another bad hangover.

He sits still, listening, waiting for something horrible. His eyes scan, dancing around the apartment.

Am I alone?

There's no sign of anyone. Not a single sound, other than the busy city below still rolling even at this hour. There are spikes of pain. Dull aches along with

TABLE 13   255

bumps and bruises, but a lot of his bandages have been removed, leaving healing wounds instead of blood and gore.

Spartacus purrs, rubbing against him. Hank pets him. A warm rush flows through him. The simplicity of a pet's affection. He sees his laptop and legal pads on the same shitty table he found on the street. The plastic trash bags he used to move his clothes here from his hometown are still on the floor by the bathroom.

Looking down, he sees something by the couch.

On the floor next to him is a Nike bag. There's a note resting on top. It's typed, no handwriting. Hank thinks of the letters Nathan and Gina sent to the restaurant to reserve a table. The note is short.

Tools to control your environment, Hank.

Hank takes a deep breath and unzips the bag. There's a Glock resting on top of rubber band-bound rolls of cash. He coughs out a laugh more like a choke.

He's never felt more lost. More unsure of anything.

He seems safe, but is he? Did she get what she wanted and moved on?

His fingers touch the gun, then the money. The feel of them gives him comfort in a sick, unnatural way. As if this fixes things. Makes all of it okay somehow.

His phone lies just under the rolls of cash. He can't believe it. She gave it back. He grabs it, scanning the texts and the calls. There are voicemails that have been listened to but not deleted. The same with the long strings of text conversations.

Hank holds his breath. Gina answered texts from his mom. From work. From Mags.

He lies back down, scrolling through them all. Reviewing his life that he didn't live. The world Gina created and manipulated, moving it all along as the mood struck her. So angry he could kill, but at the same time, so grateful that he's alive. A whirlwind of contradicting feelings.

Did she mean what she said? Separate ways?

Spartacus rubs his head against Hank's face.

His phone buzzes. It's Mags. She's texting him. Continuing a conversation Gina started. A chill runs down his spine. The thought of picking up where he left off is almost too much. Can he go back to before that night as if none of this happened? He wants to believe it's possible.

Why can't it be? Why fight hope?

He sees the time of the last text sent to Mags from his phone. Hank's heart skips a row of beats. Gina was here less than an hour ago.

TABLE 13   257

He scrolls up, reading what Gina sent.

Let's finish that bottle.

Mags's response.

Hell yes! Feeling better?

Hank takes a deep breath, letting the waterfall of emotions roll over him. Too much to handle. Jagged pieces that slice deep when putting them together. With trembling fingers, he taps out his response.

Soooo much better.

THIRTY-THREE
ONE YEAR LATER

MAGS KISSES HANK just before they step into the restaurant.

Everybody knows they're a thing, but they both agreed there was no reason to throw it in everyone's faces. So, they try to keep any and all signs of physical affection outside of the workplace. Where it probably belongs. They've both witnessed other romantically involved coworkers pawing all over one another before and decided that's not the way they wanted to play this. Work is work. Let's not manufacture a reason for people to hate us.

Mags takes her place at the hostess stand. The dinner rush is minutes away from pouring over them. Hank steps into the men's room to check his look for the evening.

When he first came back to work, he avoided the

TABLE 13   259

men's room at all costs. So much so, he would either hold it when nature called or go next door. Slowly but surely, as time passed, he got more comfortable being in here. The fear was real the first day back. Really shook him hard. But now, he hardly thinks at all about what happened here.

After a police investigation, Chef's death was ruled an accident. The autopsy revealed he was on several different meds for depression and focus, along with an apparently self-prescribed regimen of cocaine and vodka. So, slipping, falling, and snapping one's neck in a bathroom while jacked out of your skull of powder, pills, and sauce wasn't all that shocking. NYPD's words, not the official statement from restaurant management. And those security cameras, the ones that Nathan and Gina told Hank were watching the bathroom doors? Complete bullshit. Yet another fun story they took delight in telling.

Hank adjusts his tie. Aligns his belt. Washes his hands.

He hasn't thought about them in weeks. The first few nights back were rough. Horrible, to be more precise. He'd wake up screaming. Crying. Swinging at people and things that weren't there. Luckily, he was alone. He got a room at a hotel during those first few nights. His cousin came back from wherever he was and not so politely told Hank it was time to get the hell out. It was only a few hours after he woke up on the couch. Hank hopes Spartacus understands.

Hank peeled off some of the Nike bag cash from Gina and found an expensive but reasonable for the area hotel for a few nights. Using cash raised some eyebrows, but he explained he worked in the restaurant industry. Everything was understood.

He went back to work. Mags gave him the biggest hug ever. He returned to normal the best he could. Found a rhythm to his world.

Gina had sent Mags text messages along the way from his phone, telling her that he was sick, really sick, and he'd be back to work as soon as he could. Hank reviewed the conversation before he came back so that his story would match what Mags had told everyone.

Crazy to think he was only gone for ten days. The drugs they stuck him with, the way they hid sunlight from him, all made him completely unaware of time and space. Besides that, the restaurant closed for a few weeks. It was out of respect, but they were also waiting for the police investigation lose steam and for the news to fade from New Yorker's short-term memories. They did some remodeling during that time to refresh the place a bit. *A new beginning*, that kind of thing. So, it was really like Hank wasn't gone at all. They even paid the staff for the time the place

TABLE 13   261

was closed. Deep pocket owners wanted to keep staff in place in order to reduce any jarring effects on the restaurant's oh-so-important guests.

Part of Hank feels bad for never telling Mags what really happened. But the other part of him, the one that won the debate, knows there's no way to explain it all. There was a risk she'd leave, or be kind for a while, then leave after she understood Hank was damaged goods.

Deep down, he knows Mags wouldn't do that, but still, she is a human being, and he wants them to start out as close to normal as possible.

Mags and Hank did finally get to finish that delicious bottle of Angel's Envy. Eat the Rich, true to her word, kept it for them nice and safe behind the bar. While they were drinking, celebrating Hank's return and talking about everything Hank was willing to talk about, Mags found out that Hank was living at a hotel.

That night was one of the most special times of Hank's life. He hopes it was for Mags too. They went back to her place and went at each other as if it were their last night on earth. They barely got the door closed before clothes started hitting the floor. Hank never felt more alive. More present. Never felt more at one with another person. *Made love* or *fucked each other's brains out*—however one chooses to describe it, and both could apply, Hank had never done either with someone he truly cared about.

Maybe that was why it meant so much to him.

Must have meant something to Mags too. She asked if he wanted to stay at her place for a while until he figured out something more permanent than a hotel. As fate would have it, her roommate had given up on becoming an actress and left town, giving Mags about five minutes' notice. Hank said yes. They *made love/fucked each other's brains out* again.

That was about eight months ago.

He's started writing again. Got a new agent based on some new work he's done. He took what he could remember from that time spent *working* with Nathan and Gina and decided to stop fighting what he thought the world wanted from him and write the thriller/horror stuff he loved so much as a kid.

He's calling it *Table Thirteen* oddly enough. His agent told him publishers were going to eat it up with a fucking spoon. Her words, not his.

Hank checks his eyebrows in the bathroom mirror. He shuts off the water, then dries off his hands before walking out into the dining room and making that quick turn into the kitchen. Showtime is moments away. His first table of the night will be here soon. He listens to the new chef review the menu and other details the staff needs to know. Hank likes this new

TABLE 13   263

chef. She's smart and supportive, but will still kick your ass when it's required.

"Hank."

Turning around, he finds Mags standing by the walk-in freezer. She holds a funny smile.

"What's up?"

"You've got a table."

"Cool. Did they just get sat?"

"Yeah, but that's not it." Mags stops. Scrunches her nose. "It's your mom."

"What?"

Hank's mind races through his last conversation with his mom. Nothing about coming to New York. She's barely ever been out of Texas. She'd never show up unannounced.

"That's not all. You need to go out there." Mags thumbs out the door. "They're at table thirteen."

Hank stops breathing. His heart launches up into his throat.

They push out into the dining room. There at table thirteen, sits Hank's mom. Pretty as the last time he saw her. She fidgets with her dress. She looks around, fake smile, back stiff as a board. Hank can feel her discomfort from across the floor.

A crying baby in a stroller is next to his mom's leg. She pushes it gently back and forth, trying to soothe the child. Hank blinks. Starts to speak, then stops.

"Your friend came in with them." Mags motions toward the door.

Standing near the exit is Gina. Raven-haired wig. Her smile is huge.

She rubs the back of a man. A new man. Like Nathan, but different. A few years younger, slick, carved out of stone, with green eyes and olive skin. He has a scar on the side of his face that doesn't match the rest of him.

Hank feels himself peel away.

Gina waves. Mags is talking, but Hank can't hear a word that she's saying. He looks at his mom. She stands. Face frozen in fear. Like she's seen the devil. Hank knows that's exactly who she's seen.

Gina and her new man walk through the front door and out into the street. Hank moves past Mags, chasing after them. Cutting, pushing past guests, he makes it out onto the busy New York street. It's early evening. The sun has begun shutting down for the day. People hurry back and forth in front of him.

His head jerks left and right. His body turns, spinning in small circles while he searches for them. Panic taking hold. He can't find them.

"Hank."

The sound of her voice sends gooseflesh up his arm. Turning around, Gina is standing only a few feet from him. He can smell her. He remembers the smell

TABLE 13   265

of her perfume from the house. Her new green-eyed man stands by the street, a car door open, tapping his wrist, indicating it is time to go.

"We've got a thing." She thumbs toward the car. "Ya know? You remember *things*, right? Still got a great video of you doing a *thing*. Parking garage, if memory serves—"

"What are you doing? You said—"

"I say all kinds of shit, Hank. Don't be a baby."

"Gina. We need to go," her man says.

She holds up a finger. He stands down.

"He's sweet but impatient as hell. Known him for years. We work well together." She makes that sound with her mouth. "He needed someone. So did I. Here we are. Kinda beautiful, right?"

As she drifts toward the open car door, Hank's legs go weak. He wants to chase after them. Slam her head into that car door until her body goes limp. But he doesn't. He stands there like a statue watching, waiting to see what she does to his world next. The one she's held in her hand since that night.

Gina stops, shakes her head, then rushes back over to him. Hugs him tight and then releases with a quick jolt.

"Take care of our little guy, will you?" She taps his nose. "Sorry. I tried. Just wasn't as fun as I thought it would be."

"You can't do this."

"Sure I can. You must not be paying attention."

She hands him a roll of cash. Pauses, then hands him another.

"Again, sorry this didn't work out as discussed, but the kid is partly your product, and he really does not fit into my environment. So…"

As she walks to the car, she kisses her new man on the cheek.

"Be careful with all that. The boy…" She stops. Lip curls. "He's a killer. You can see it. Just like his old man."

Hank realizes how right she may be. That child is part him and part her.

Gina and her new man slide into the car. The door shuts. The car takes off, disappearing into the sea of yellow cabs, limos, and rideshare worker bees. Hank stands stuck in the street. The throngs of people move past and around him. A stone stuck in a raging river.

He plays with the rolls of cash. Thinks of the other ones he has left in that shoebox he keeps from Mags. So much he's kept from her. This is the life he has. The one he's chosen, mixed with what's been chosen for him.

Mags and his mom step out of the restaurant.

His mom holds the baby. He's stopped crying.

TABLE 13   267

Hank looks to Mags. So many questions surely in her mind. Where to begin? Should he even try?

He could run.

He has money. He can go anywhere.

He can slip out into this crowd of everything and everyone, get the cash from Mags's apartment and become a ghost in no time flat. That's what Gina would do. She is the alpha. A world in which everyone she meets becomes a product of her.

Hank looks into Mags's eyes.

Thinks of that first night, their first maybe date. He looks to his mom. All she's been through with him. For him. Then there's the baby. His baby with Gina. Is that child a killer? A time bomb of everything bad Gina and Hank are?

Maybe. Maybe not.

Maybe a good, loving home can override the bad. Not that Hank would know anything about what a good, loving home looks like. The questions roll in like the tide. Getting closer and closer with each crashing wave.

Gina has a video of him killing people.

Can he explain any of this insanity to Mags and his mom? After the lies he's told them both over the last year? Will they accept any of it? Will they leave him all alone in the world?

Maybe his mom will stick with him. Hell, this isn't the worst she's dealt with.

But will Mags? Why would she?

Her face is a question mark. God only knows what stories she's come up with to fill in the blanks over the last few minutes.

"Hank?" His mom's voice is soaked in worry. "Hank, honey?"

His world shuts down. He lied to himself and to everyone else over the last year, saying everything was fine. Better than before.

Denial at peak level.

No matter what happens, no matter what he does, his choices are not his to make. As hard as it is to rationalize, losing control is almost liberating. Understanding it all is pointless. Acceptance will slowly but surely find a way in. Always does. However, at this moment, one thing is understood with absolute certainty.

His world, and everything in it, belongs to someone else.

HOPE YOU LIKED TABLE 13

Thank you for reading, and I hope you enjoyed the ride. I'm always amazed and humbled by the kindness of readers.

Please take a moment and leave an honest review. They are an unbelievable help, and it will only take a second or two. Your opinion matters, but only if you share it.

Review Table 13

Thank you,
Mike

ALSO BY MIKE McCRARY

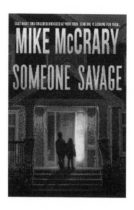

**Last night two children knocked at his door.
Someone is looking for them...**

Nicholas Hooper wanted to be left alone. Looking
to escape his past and his unfortunate present, the
best-selling author rented a luxury house in the
Poconos to finish what very well could be his very
last book. But his plans change when one night he
opens his front door to find two frightened
children.

A young girl and boy all alone. They refuse to
speak. Looking for help.

Hooper takes them into town to see if the local
police can help uncover the mystery of what has
happened to these children. But what happens next

is something Hooper never saw coming. The children are escaping their past too and their present is far worse than anything Hooper could have ever imagined. Can Hooper battle his own personal demons and protect these innocent children?

Someone Savage is a page-turning thriller packed with shocking twists and heart-stopping suspense. If you like Harlan Coben, Karin Slaughter, and Rachel Abbott then you'll love best-selling author Mike McCrary's gripping tale.

"I was hooked from page one." ★★★★★ Review

"It had everything and more." ★★★★★ Review

"A very exciting novel with plenty of twists and turns - thrilling from start to finish." ★★★★★ Review

"Oh my god!! I have just finished reading this rollercoaster of a book." ★★★★★ Review

"You are caught up in his nightmare right away, hurrying to turn pages..." ★★★★★ Review

ACKNOWLEDGMENTS

After every book, I say the same thing.

You can't do a damn thing alone.

And it's true every time—that's why I say it—and it's so, so true with this book as well. There are a lot of great people that have helped me with this crazy little writing life.

But this time around, I'd like to do something a little different.

A good friend of mine passed away recently. He was, without question, one of the best people I've ever known. He had this thing he'd say. He used to say, "Leave a room better than you found it." I know it's a cliché of sorts when someone dies to call them a great light. But Jason Kiehl was a great light. A world-class, life of the party kinda fella. He owned a laugh and a smile that you wanted to be around. He made every room a better place to be.

He was all those things and more, but he was also kind. Kind enough to read a friend's books. Jason read almost all of my books, and he would always call me so we could talk about them. Sure, we'd mix in conversations and jokes about life, the good old days, and whatever else. But he always called to talk about the stories. What he liked about the characters. What made him cringe. What made him smile.

It makes me incredibly sad to think that I won't have that conversation about this book or any books, but I feel a tremendous amount of gratitude that I had those conversations. That I was allowed to have that time even though I had no idea how precious it was.

Like I said, Jason had a great laugh and an incredible sense of humor. Like no one I've ever met. One time, after reading my latest book, Jason told me he loved the new stuff but missed some of the old stuff. He said, and this is a quote, "Dude. It's cool, but I miss all the profanity in Remo." Well, Jason, this is for you...

Shit. Fuck. Dick. Fuck-stick. Dickhole.

Butt plug. Fuck-face. Suck-butt. Assclown. Twat.

Dipshit-piece-of-shit-motherfucker.

Snot. Balls.

Rest in peace, Jason. Love you, brother.

ABOUT THE AUTHOR

Mike has been a waiter, securities trader, dishwasher, investment manager, and an unpaid Hollywood intern. He's quit corporate America, come back, been fired, been promoted, been fired, and currently, from his home in Texas, he writes stories about questionable people making questionable decisions.

Keep up with Mike at...
www.mikemccrary.com
mccrarynews@mikemccrary.com

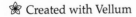